TREVOR

STRONG MANOR Book 6

KATHI S. BARTON

World Castle Publishing, LLC
Pensacola, Florida
Copyright © 2025 Kathi S. Barton
Hardback ISBN: 9798314630495
Paperback ISBN: 9798891263659
eBook ISBN: 9798891263666
First Edition World Castle Publishing, LLC, March 19, 2025
http://www.worldcastlepublishing.com

Licensing Notes

Cover: Karen Fuller
Editor: Karen Fuller

Prologue

LeAnn watched her ward play on the floor in front of the television. The stupid thing hadn't worked for about a month now, but it didn't seem that either one of them missed it all that much. She was happy that the little girl had been with her when her mother had been killed. LeAnn oftentimes wondered if anyone knew that Prissy had had a child, much less one as pretty and as young as little Debra was.

She was sure that, at some point, someone would have come for her had they known about her. LeAnn had started sleeping with a gun in her hand when they went to bed, the little girl in the bed next to her. But when she nearly blew a hole in the electrical man who read the meter, she decided that she might well be better off hiding them all over the house. It had broken her heart, too, that she'd had to show little Debra how to use it and how to be safe around it.

"Grannie?" She asked the child what she

could do for her, smiling each time she heard her calling her such a sweet name. "There's a man at the door. Did you hear him?" She said that she'd not and told her to go and hide. "Yes, ma'am. I'll go hide. But you be extra careful, please. I don't have nobody but you in my life."

For an eight-year-old, the child was beyond smart. It took her very little time to teach the child that things weren't like other people's homes and that she had to be extra quiet when anyone came around. Looking around her sparse rooms, LeAnn thought she was about as ready as she could be for a visitor. She only hoped that they weren't there for Debra. Being as old as she was, there wasn't much fight left in her to keep her safe much longer.

"Hello, Ms. Jamestown. My name is David Westminster. I'm from the power and light company." She asked him what he wanted. "Well, if I could come in, I'd be able to show you how we're able to save you about a hundred dollars a month on your bills."

"I don't pay but about half that now. If'n you're going to be able to save me a hundred, am I gonna get to keep the other fifty?" He laughed, it was forced, but she knew it when she'd opened the door that he was out for trouble. "You go on now.

Leave this old woman alone. I got me enough to worry about what with the neighbor's dog coming over all the time and eating my tomatoes in the summer months. Go on now."

"Where is she, LeAnn?" She asked him what he was speaking about. "The girl, the child of your daughter? I know you have her. Just let me have her, and I'll make sure you never have to go without again."

"Oh, for the love of Pete. If'n I had a daughter, you dumb cracker, don't you think I'd know it? I'm pretty near ninety years old now. A daughter of mine would be in her seventies. Even a kid of hers would be in their fifties if she was to have a kid herself. Where do you get off...I done already told you to go on now. I ain't got no daughter. And if'n I had one, she would never have been considered a child. I'm sure to Christ, she'd be an old and ugly one."

He shoved at the door just as she heard the back door open. She was scared beyond words now and let herself fall to the floor when he knocked her back. There was a gun just there under the footstool, and as soon as she got to it, she was going to —

"Mrs. Jamestown? It's Trevor Strong. I'm

here to help you out with the paperwork. Are you here?" She knew that she should have known the name, but she was too afraid to think beyond the men in her house. LeAnn told the man who was still calling for her that she was in the living room being shoved around. The big man who came in through the mud room winked at her. Making her feel like she was just a young girl and he'd come to courtin. "My dad, you know him, Barkley? He said that you prefer when someone comes into the back door like company. I'm assuming that this fellow here isn't company nor welcome."

"No, sir, he's not. Come in here telling me that he knows about some child that I have of my daughters or some story. I'm nearly ninety, the young fool. If I had me a young person working around here, don't you think that I'd have a much nicer and certainly cleaner place? I swear to Jon, people just don't think with their minds no more. That's what it is. Nobody is thinking beyond what they want to hear." She looked the young man over as he helped her up from the floor. The other man, still with his gun out, told Trevor that he'd been here first. "Well, you might well have been first, but you didn't even bother helping an old woman up from the floor. You even knocking me there didn't have you helping me out."

She was babbling. She knew that. Her heart was hurting her, and she wanted to get to her nitro pills before it became a full-bloom pain. Reaching for the tiniest little bottle she thought the drugstore had, she knocked it to the floor and knew that she was going to just die right then.

"Here, you go. Let me help you out with that." Not only did he get her pill bottle picked up, but he had the little sucker open and was putting an equally tiny pill under her tongue. Almost as soon as it melted, she could feel it working. Trevor even told her that in a minute, if she wasn't better, he had her a second one, too. LeAnn nearly sobbed. Nobody had been around to help her but the child and she just didn't know what to say.

Leaning her head back on her chair after getting the second little pill, LeAnn closed her eyes and let the two men argue about the silliest things. At least to her befuddled mind, it seemed like they weren't making nary a bit of sense. It scared her a bit, feeling this way. She couldn't leave the child alone, not until she was able to talk to someone about her and why she was hiding her.

LeAnn must have dozed off for a bit there because the next time she opened her eyes, Debra was helping her with a sip or two of water and asking her if she needed another pill. Taking it, just to be sure that everything in her chest was working the way that it was supposed to, she was glad to see that the big man, she couldn't remember his name at the moment, was on the telephone. Since she knew for a fact that he'd not been on her house phone, LeAnn figured that he had one of them cellular phones that he was using. She looked at Debra when she called out to her.

"That man had the password to make me come up out of the cellar. He said that he was going to call his daddy and get us to a safer place. Are you all right?" She said that she was and that Barkley, his daddy, was her friend. "That man that was here when I went downstairs, he's fit to be tied standing on the street with the police. They arrested him on account of him having a gun when he was on parole. He sure was powerful upset that Mr. Strong came in and ruined his plans. He didn't say what they were, but the police hauled him right out of here kicking and screaming about how he was here to get a little girl."

"I don't know how he ever thought that you'd not be prepared for someone coming alone, do you, Mrs. J?" She smiled at the nickname, remembering him as a young man when he'd come here with his daddy sometimes. "Dad told me to tell you that he's sending his best men here to make sure you get out of here all in one piece. Debra here is going to be as safe as we can make her too."

"They want her on account of them thinking that she knows more than her mother did. You know she's not my granddaughter, don't you, son?" He said that he did and that he remembered being around here when she had baked him some chocolate chip cookies. "Yes, I remember that. You sure could eat your weight in them."

They both laughed, and she felt her heart tensing up a little bit again. Not taking a third pill, she told Debra to make sure that she got her mother's books from the cellar. While she was down there, she looked at the young man who seemed to know just what she was going to say to him.

"You hang on now. My dad said that you owe him a game of chess." She said she didn't know if she could remember how to play now. "An ambulance is coming to get you. Now, don't you be frightened when they zip you up in one of those body bags. Ms. J. Debra will be in there with you, holding onto you for dear life. Don't frighten her by doing something sad, all right?"

"I hurt, and I'm old." He said that he was going to make sure that she got herself some good care. "I know, Trevor, but I've only been holding on for the last few years until someone came along and helped me out while caring for little Debra. She's not a bit of trouble, but I'm ninety years old. My poor old body just can't hold on too much longer."

"My dad is going to meet the two of you at the hospital. I know you have things to tell him. Things that the two of you have been putting your heads together about for a long time. Now, you just hang on until then, and everyone will be happy. You're not going to believe it, Ms. J but my brothers are all married now with babies and children coming along. You have to hang on a bit to see them all. Please?" She cried, and she watched him as fat tears rolled down his own cheeks. Trevor had always been a good boy and she so hated to disappoint him. "Will you at least try for me, please?"

"I'll try, young man, but I expect you to be there when I'm passing on. I need a young person to hold onto my hand when I'm passing over into the next world. It'll make me ease into it better whilst I look for my husband. Now that I think on it, he's been gone longer than we were married. Probably got him a whole lot of women just hanging on his every word." They both laughed, and she felt another pain rip right through her. "It ain't gonna be long, Trevor. You make sure that your daddy knows that."

He said that he would and went to let in the medics. It had been forever since she'd had so many guests in her home, and she didn't have nary a cookie or cup of coffee to offer them. When they got her onto the gurney, feeling the nice mattress under her worn-out body, they told her that they were going to give her a bit of something that would make her feel a lot better.

Sure enough, it did. Her heart was beating at its full strength, and she felt just a little like she could take on the world. After a bit, when they told her that she seemed to be steady, they had little Debra lay over her gentle like, and then they put the biggest sheet over the two of them like she was being carted away to the funeral parlor.

They strapped the two of them down, and she might have been a little afeared of the darkness, but Debra started to sing to her, a little song that she'd picked up off the television when it had been working, and she sang along with her. People might well have been scared out of fifty years of their lives if'n they heard that big old sheet covering them singing about the colors of the world. She smiled a bit. Debra could certainly make her feel like she'd had a good long time left in her old body. She surely did.

Once they were at the hospital, they were taken to an elevator and told that they only had a little bit more. She heard Trevor's voice talking to someone, and she felt a might better about it. There was someone with him, a doctor he called him, and he was telling the other man what he'd done in the way of helping Ms. J make it here.

"I'd like for her to be around a bit longer if you think you can make that work for us." The doctor said he'd give it his all as he thought the world of Lisa and Barkley Strong. "They like you too, Jimson. I heard that you were excited about the new equipment that my brother and sister have been working on."

When the elevator stopped, she was ready to get off the mattress. It had gone from feeling just fine to something that didn't have nary a soft spot in it. As soon as she was put on a better bed, her whole self felt like she'd been given a million-dollar place to rest her head. But it wasn't doing all that much for her heart. She was never so glad to see Barkley Strong as she was in that moment.

"I fear I don't have too much longer to go, sir. I just can't seem to keep this ticker here going." Barkley told her that he had her. "Good, you always were the best of the best of the best when you'd come over and mow my lawn. Now, you listen to me better than you did in them flower lessons I gave you. Didn't I tell you that they'd come in handy?"

She told him everything. LeAnn knew that she was getting close to the end of her talking and her body being around. But it was as important to her to tell him everything that he'd need to know as it was for her to make sure that he knew all about it. Debra, she came and held her hand off and on, the little mite crying a great deal, but she too knew what was going to happen to her, and she was surprised every day that she opened her eyes that she was in this life for another day or two.

"You got them books I been sending you?" He said that he also had the ones that were in her cellar. "That child, she'll know where to find everything else you might need too. You keep her safe, Barkley. That little thing is smarter than anyone I've done ever did know, including you."

"You know that I'll keep her more than safe, Ms. J." No one will ever find her, not so long as there is breath in my body." She closed her eyes but opened them off and on to make sure that they were all still there and if'n they had any questions to put to her. While she wasn't all that sure she could answer them, she knew that someone would be there to listen to her.

"Grannie?" She had to focus really hard on seeing who was talking to her and when that pretty little thing smiled at her, it hurt her bad that she couldn't remember her name. "It's Debra. I wanted to tell you that I love you with all my heart. And that I'm sure that I'm only alive because of you."

"Aren't you the sweetest little thing? I think, and we both know it, that you could have done this all on your own without me meddling in your life." Debra laid her head on her chest. It wasn't hurting now. None of her old body was. "You make sure you listen to everything that Barkley and his family tell you, child. They'll keep you out of harm's way. All right?"

"Yes, ma'am, I know that." LeeAnn closed her eyes and couldn't pry them open again when

Debra, that was her name, said something to her. "You go on now, Grannie. You don't have to make sure I have beans and taters anymore. Go on now and go in peace."

"I think I will. I surely did love you, child." She thought that she told her that she loved her too but couldn't be sure. LeAnn was as sure of her love for the child as she had been her husband nearly sixty years ago now. "You be good, honey. I'll see you when you come a calling."

~*~

Trevor had no idea what made him stop at the little house that was so far off the road that few people even knew that it was back there. When he'd seen the man on the front porch, he'd made his way around to the back to make sure that Ms. J wasn't being ambushed. As it was, he had to break into the house, knocking the window out of the mudroom to gain access. He didn't know what he'd find when he got inside, but his heart was telling him that she needed him, and Trevor was never one to second guess himself when his mind or heart was talking to him.

He'd been afraid when he'd seen the elderly woman on the floor. More so to see the man standing over her yelling about the child. He did know that Ms. J had someone living with her, but he'd not known who it was—actually, he still didn't—until he remembered the password that he'd been given long ago to get the person to trust him.

When Debra came out of the cellar, cobwebs were not only all over her jeans but in her hair as well. He helped her clean up while she told him what was going on. The man, he'd not caught his name was gone now, the police having come to get him just after Trevor had broken into the house. As soon as he could, he called his dad and mom to tell them that he wasn't sure that Ms. J was going to make it after telling them what he'd come up upon when he'd pulled in behind the house. His dad told him that he was on his way and Trevor told him to drive safely but to hurry. Turned out he was right to have his dad hurry it along. The elderly woman died not ten minutes after they got her to a hospital room.

"Mr. Trevor?" He asked Debra again just to call him Trevor. "Grannie said that I wasn't to trust anyone but your dad. I don't know what it is about you, but I have the same trust for you that I have for him." He got down to her level before speaking to her again.

"My dad and I used to come here a lot before you came here. Then, one day, we came here, and Ms. J had a tiny little baby in her arms. I know you don't remember that but I got to hold you for hours while they talked business. You were then and are now a pretty little thing." She thanked him. "Did you know how you ended up with her? I mean, I know that she didn't have any living children and that most people didn't have all that much to do with her. Thinking that she was an oddball. She wasn't. Just a lovely woman that didn't take crap from anyone."

"It's in those books why I was with her. I don't know, to be honest. I wasn't to read the books that she'd had in the cellar. I could read the new ones, but not those." He had a feeling that if asked she could recite the entirety of all the books if asked. "Grannie, she wasn't my relative at all. But I had to hide out when people came around sniffing. It took me a long time to figure out what that meant. She had funny words for things that I had to come to understand."

"Yes, I had a grandda like that too. He could say things that would make you scratch your head and more than likely still not have any idea what he was talking about. Even when I got older, I still didn't know." They both laughed, and he and her moved to the living room in his parents' home. He'd never been so relaxed around a child before. "From what my dad told me about you, is that your some kind of prodigy. Is that right?"

"Yes." When she didn't say anymore he didn't ask. Whatever she was smart about, he figured that he'd find out soon or later or not. Really, it wasn't any of his business. Dad had it under control, and he was fine with that.

They talked about Halloween for a little while. Of course, she'd never been trick or treating. Nor had she had a big Thanksgiving dinner with family around. Grannie, she told him, would get food delivered to the house all the time, and they'd share it. Also, they had them a nice-sized garden that they'd eat from all summer and into the fall year. Debra told him how Grannie had taught her the basics of canning and that she could live in the forest for months so long as she had a sharp knife and a bottle. He figured out what the knife was for easily, but she explained to him what the bottle was for.

"Carrying stuff. Toting things back and forth that I'd find to eat or need. Also, it was nice to have water brought to wherever I was hiding out.

Each summer since I was three, grannie would tell me to go away and not come back for a month. She wanted me to be able to care for myself in the event that something happened to her. I guess she was right. I'm going to miss her so much." Trevor told her how sorry he was and held her while she cried. "It was fun, honestly. And I did learn a great deal. I can find things in the forest to keep my belly filled up that nobody I know would think about. I would always get to have cake, something that we rarely had when I was with her."

He could see that, too. Someone like Grannie, her age, giving the child answers to questions about the outdoors that she'd not get from a book or someone younger. Her relationship with her, too, someone watching over her that would be better than any other relationship that she'd have with a parent who wasn't around or even one who didn't care if she needed help or not. Debra told him that she'd learned how to know where she was at any given time, too, so she'd be able to find her way home. He did wonder why she was taught those things, wondering what kind of scary things Ms. J knew about the little girl.

"She's going to be staying with your mother and me until we can get things figured out with the government. If you'd not mind, I don't want either of you to say anything to anyone until we know for sure that we can trust them. Of course, your brothers and their wives will know. However, as far as anyone else is concerned, she's just a relative who is spending the holidays with us until such time as her parents return. That's all the information that anyone needs to know. If they get too pushy, well, I'll have Jade or Jenson take care of them." Both he and Debra laughed. "As soon as that came out of my mouth, I knew it was the wrong thing to say. Anyway, once we get something more than we have now, we'll be able to move forward."

"The man that was at the house today, he seemed really pushy. What happened to him?" Dad just looked at him and didn't answer Debra. "Okay, so I'm assuming that it's best if I don't know. I can live with that. I'm not sure, but I think that Grannie took care of a couple of pushy people, too. I helped her put them in the well at the back of the property. I won't be getting into trouble over that, will I?"

Dad told Debra that he'd look into it, but he shivered when he said it. Trevor, too, had a feeling that there wouldn't be just a couple of bodies back there but as many as six. The way that the police were talking earlier, there had been some kind of trouble going on here for a long time.

When Jade showed up, she told Dad that she'd gone shopping and had some things for Debra. After she took off to try some of them on, she looked at the two of them like she had some serious information to hand out. He wasn't entirely positive that he wanted to hear it but sat down when she told him to. Christ, all he'd done was check on an elderly lady that he'd met long ago, and now he was knee-deep in whatever was going on with a child.

"The elderly Jamestown had some traces of poison in her body. I'm not saying that the child did it, but I'd be extra careful around her if I were you." Dad asked if he'd be all right here with her then. "I would say so. If I were you, I'd have Trevor move in here too, another set of eyes that can watch over things. It might well not be her that did it, but I'm not taking any chances with either of you." Dad looked at him.

"I can stay here, you know that, for as long as you need. However, I haven't any idea how I'm supposed to keep an eye on someone so that they don't poison you. I mean, I'm not a stupid man, but that's well beyond anything that I studied for in college." Dad said that just having him here would be a blessing. "You know that I'd give my life for you and Mom. Just tell me when you want me here, and I'll—"

"Tonight." He nodded and worked around in his head on how to move things around on his schedule so that he could work with his parents and not miss too much in the way of working.

Then he felt stupid for doing that, making work first in his life, so he decided that he'd clear his calendar until his parents no longer needed him. As Jade was leaving, she handed him a thumb drive. She didn't say a word, of course, but kissed him on the cheek and whispered to him to use his own laptop. This was getting scarier and scarier all the time.

~*~

Trevor didn't care for the little girl. He wasn't one to make snap judgments about people, but there was something decidedly creepy about the kid. Even Sherm, the nicest kid he'd ever met, seemed to not want to have much to do with her. Debra Carter was odd. Not only that but she was snippy, as his mom would call it.

No one knew that the child was with him.

Well, not him, but his parents. Sherm was the only kid who knew that she was around, and he wouldn't tell. He was the most adult child that he'd ever met and trusted him more than he did his own banker.

"She's weird." He told Sherm that wasn't nice. "Well, she is. Last night, I asked her if she wanted to play a game on my reader, and she told me that it would melt my brain. I might be younger than her, but I know better than that."

"Sherm, you're younger than I am, and you know a lot of things that I don't. But you found out her age?" He told him that she told him that she was twelve. "You say that like you don't believe it. You think she's older or younger?"

"I don't know, to be honest. She's just weird." Sherm had been telling him that for the past three days. It was like he didn't know what other label to put on the girl. While Mrs. J had left them notes on the child, there really wasn't enough personal information about her to be able to know where she came from or how she had ended up at Mrs. J's home.

Then there was the thumb drive that he'd been given. He no more understood that than he did how a kid could be so smart with the dumbest parents around. Correcting himself. He knew how that happened. Sherm was a product of a good home. Just yesterday, he'd been talking to someone at his office who said that their child had been tested and was considered gifted.

"She's reading off the charts in books. Only ten years old and reading at a high school age. Can you believe it?" He was reasonably sure that he wasn't supposed to answer no at that point. "I just can't believe how smart my little girl is."

Neither did he. He had attempted to converse with the child, who appeared to be an ordinary kid at first glance. However, when he offered her a book, she didn't settle down to read as expected. Instead, she fidgeted restlessly, tearing out pages and eating them. Unless she was somehow absorbing the book's contents through her mouth, he doubted she could read at all.

After spending what little time he did with Debra, he realized that she was forever staring at things. Not like looking, he looked at things and observed. But she would go off in this kind of trance and stare at something for a good hour before she'd look back at him. Trevor shivered. That just creeped him out, too.

"Did you know that there are tests that you

can give someone to see what sort of intelligence they have?" Sherm told him all about the tests he'd taken them several times and what they would tell you about a gifted person. "It…Grandma said I can't call her an "it" anymore. She might be only gifted in one thing. Like I am. I can read, hear, or smell something, and I will remember it forever. But I've applied my gift, I guess you can call it, so that I can use it to help others. There are some kids who can do math and see things beyond the scope that it is. I can do that too but I have to have something to draw it out so that it doesn't get all fuzzy in my head."

"What do you think Debra is gifted with?" He told him, again, that she was just weird. "Sherm, I don't think that's a gift. Being weird, I mean. What would that even be?" But the more he thought about it, he thought that was what she was gifted with. Being weird.

Trevor hadn't been able to talk to Jade or any of the others about the girl or the thumb drive. He'd watched it from beginning to end several times, and he no more understood what he was looking at then than he did a book on political science that Jenson had given him. It might as well have been in a different language as far as he was concerned.

There were other things about the girl, too. She had a habit, well, he wasn't sure it was a habit or not, something else that made her weird, he supposed, but she wouldn't eat things on her plate that touched something else.

Like she'd not eat succotash. The corn and the lima beans touching were too much for her. All her food was put into separate bowls or plates. And she would need a new fork with each thing, too. The other night, she'd had a meltdown because he'd put mushrooms on her steak. She had wanted both, but he'd not known about the touching thing until then. Dad had to leave the room, and Mom… well, she seemed like she thought the kid was… weird. Like Sherm had said.

Also, she wouldn't wear socks with her shoes. She'd wear them around the house, keeping her feet cozy inside of them, but once she had to put on shoes, nope, she'd take them off and put them in the laundry.

As he was eating his lunch, making sure that everything on his paper plate touched, he had to laugh when his Mom sat down beside him and told him to behave. As if she knew just what he was up to. After kissing her on the cheek and offering her the last of his chips, she took one bite and picked up his drink.

"You could have warned me." After she drank down most of what was left in his paper cup she made him go and get her a refill. While he was there, he also got her a bottle of water. Setting both down in front of her, he watched as she tried to get rid of the flaming hot taste in her mouth. "What am I going to do with you, Trevor? Some woman is going to come along, take one bite of your dinner, and run to the hills."

"Nah, she'll have to get used to it. But I don't need another woman in my life. I have all I need right here with you." She smacked him on his arm. "What are you doing in this part of town? Not that I'm complaining, I love seeing you, but you don't usually come down here unless you need…did that girl say something to you?"

"She's odd, don't you think? But no, she didn't say anything to me. I don't know what to do with her most of the time." Trevor almost told his mom not to be alone with her, but he didn't. He had no idea where that thought came from but he knew it was true as much as his love for his mom. "I came into town to have lunch with Jade, but she's in the middle of a huge project. Jenson is working on his office in DC. And Grace had already eaten by the time I was able to run her down. I felt so lonely."

"I have an idea that both Jenson and Jade will be gone for the rest of the day. She told me that Jenson has some furniture that he needs to move. Grace told me that she had puppies. I'm not entirely sure what that means, but I didn't ask. I love her to pieces, but she sometimes talks like she's been having a conversation with you for several hours and that you just need to catch up with her. Also, and this one really floored me. What the heck is a Flintstone? She did mention it was an old cartoon, but I've never heard of it."

Mom was laughing. He was happy to see it; she'd been down a bit for the last few days, and when she explained to him what the Flintstone reference was, she had him look it up and watch one of the cartoons that she had enjoyed as a child.

"Oh my, Trevor, you do my heart a lot of good. I'm so happy I came to find you." She chuckled a bit more before she asked him what the puppies meant. "Do you think that it's code for something? It would be like her to come up with something like that. I just love that girl. She's forever making me have to think hard and then laugh just as hard. I believe that her sense of humor is just as good as Jade's sarcasm."

The two of them decided to go by to see Gracie. Pulling into the drive, they were amazed to see a truck backing up to the garage. Wondering what they had ordered now, the two of them bypassed the garage and made their way into the house.

The barking started first. Then the cutest little puppies, all of them round and fat, came running to them. Gracie, chasing them, yelled for us to close the door or they'd escape again had Trevor closing the door and then sitting on the floor to get as much loving as he could get from the rambunctious bunch.

After telling them how she'd ended up with the ten little beasts, she said that it had been so much fun watching them grow into their own personalities. But then, she explained that she'd only had them a few days and was still getting used to them.

"Are you going to sell them?" The look Grace gave him had him raising his hands in defense. I was just asking. Because if you are, I want my pick of them. Christ, this is like having a bundle of love right here in your hands."

"I'm not sure what I'm going to do with them all. I don't want to part with them, they give me so much joy all the time when I'm here alone, but I've only just realized today how much it's going to cost for us to feed them when they get full-sized. The vet told us that they were going to be big dogs and would need a lot of yard to play in. I have that, we have it all fenced in as well, but we've had to have the local store bring us food for them on a semi." That explained the truck in the garage. "Yes, I know. I might well have gone a little overboard with that but we won't run out anytime soon. It's difficult for me to bring home fifty-pound bags of dog food by myself weekly."

"I'll take two." She asked him if he was serious. "Yes. I want to…do you know their sex yet? If so, I want to take a male and a female. I'll have them both fixed, but I think that a brother and sister will have fun growing up together. I know that I'll enjoy it."

Trevor didn't even mind that they had names. He figured that if Gracie was willing to part with two of them for him that he'd leave their names for them. Pebbles and Bamm-Bamm were going to go home with him, along with their beds, food, and collars. Christ, he thought to himself, he was nuts but was going to enjoy this so much.

By the time Maverick made it home, his other brothers and their families showed up to get to know the newest additions to the family. Sherm wanted one so badly that it hurt him to know that he couldn't. At least not until they got their yard fenced in as well. When all was said and done, Gracie was left with two of the dogs, Fred and Wilma, so that she could watch them grow up as well.

"I have something to tell you guys since you're all here." Maverick raised his glass of tea up, tapped it with a spoon, and smiled. "Grace and I are going to have a baby in June. By then, we're hoping that the dogs will be able to be around them without falling over."

The dogs were clumsy. But so adorable. When he asked Dad if he was going to take one, he said he had enough on his plate right now with Debra. He didn't sound any more thrilled with the girl than his mom had. Trevor decided right then that he was going to dig deeper into the girl's life and find out firstly what was wrong with her and secondly why it was so important to keep her hidden away.

Something very telling was that not one of

the puppies would go near her. Blackie, the pup that seemed to be in charge of the others, just stared at the young girl and barked. In doggie language, he was sure that he told his little family that they were to avoid her. Having a dog, just a little one to avoid someone, told him that he couldn't put off any longer what he should have done by now. See what the fuck was her issue.

When he got home that night, after walking the dogs around the yard, Trevor decided that he was going to have to move into something bigger than the one-bedroom condo. They didn't have any kind of rules as to having pets, but he couldn't see that they'd be able to run around as much as they might need to when they got older.

Deciding that he didn't want a mansion like the others had but something with a couple of bedrooms and a nice yard. It was the yard that he wanted most. Something that was his and his alone. He realized that he was sick to death of sharing the space with about fifty other people.

That night, after the pups settled down, he got on the computer to have a look around. Nothing on Debra as yet. He'd do that later but to find him a home. As he was sitting on the floor, where he did his best work, he thought, the pups came over to him and cuddled up on his lap. He found himself so relaxed with them snoring gently by him that he was going to go to bed.

Something was up with the girl. He didn't know what, but he was going to find it, and if it turned out badly, anything that made her a threat to his family, he was going to make sure that she was never found. That was his job, after all.

Chapter 1

Trevor was in the yard watching his puppies playing in the snow when Jenson pulled into his driveway. He had a hard time remembering if he had a meeting with him or not today when he hugged him like he'd not seen in just yesterday.

"We're having dinner tonight with the family. Please tell me that you're going to be there." He said that he was and asked him what they were having. "I don't know yet. Mom said she had it all taken care of, so that's all I know. I'm thinking that it's going to be take away rather than cooking. They're loving living in their new home. I know that I'm happy that our house is finally finished now, and we don't have contractors all around us."

"I'm supposed to look at a few houses today. I'm not thrilled about it, to be honest. I hate the fact that I have to do this when I have other things to do but I do need a bigger place with my own yard. I want my own yard more than I do a house, you understand?" Jenson told him that he understood perfectly. "No offense, but what are you doing here? Aren't you supposed to be in DC for meetings and crap?"

"They ended the secession early today. I couldn't stand to not be at home for another minute so I hitched a ride with one of the men coming to talk to Clay. He's been doing some upgrades to the equipment that is in the NASA offices. Did he tell you that he got a bonus for getting something taken care of in space? I only half listen to him sometimes. I should pay more attention, but I get something stuck in my head and I can't understand what he's telling me. Jade knows, of course, but I tune them out when they're together. They'd never have a conversation with me around asking them to explain things to me. Even though I'm an engineer, I have trouble...my job is taking more time from me than I thought it would." Trevor asked him if it was that serious. "No. Yes. I'm not sure. I want to be with my wife. When I started out with this congress thing, I didn't have her in my life. Now? Well, all I can think about is how much I miss her and our son."

"You're in charge, aren't you? I mean, can't you say when you're going to leave or stay?"

Jenson told him that it didn't work like that. "I guess I can understand why you'd need to be hanging around there a great deal. It's something that you've always wanted. Has that changed for you?"

"Yes and no. I love what I'm doing, but like I said, I miss Jade and our kid. He's getting to the point where he's not sleeping all the time. Last night, he rolled over by himself, and both Jade and I laughed until we cried, scaring Benson until he was upset."

Taking the puppies in the house, he put them in the cage that he'd purchased for them when he'd lost one of them in the condo. He'd not really been lost, but he'd been so far under the bed sleeping that he'd not found him for a while, and it had terrified him that the little sucker had gotten out. Changing his clothing for something better, Jenson said he'd go with him to look at the houses. He was really glad for the company.

"This first house is supposed to make me realize how much I don't want a small house. I have no idea what that's supposed to mean. I've been living in a two-bedroom condo since I was eighteen years old." They pulled into the driveway, neither of them getting out. "This house is supposed to have three bedrooms, a living room, and a kitchen. I don't know that even one of my pups could live in that it's so small."

The two of them talked about how much he was looking for in a house. While he didn't want a huge assed house like they had, he didn't want to be tripping all over himself either by having the puppies, soon to be two overgrown dogs making him fall all the time.

The second house wasn't something that he wanted either. First of all, it was too close to the school, and he thought that he'd never have any peace. He did want to live closer to his parents but didn't want to have to time things so he'd not hear kids screaming all the time.

"You don't like kids?" He told his brother that he liked them just fine when they were someone else's. "That's just not right. All of the women want to have several children, and you just want to be the favorite uncle who has money to burn on them. I see how you are."

"I'm sure that there might be a person out there for me. I'm very sure of it. But I'm in no hurry to settle down and be domesticated. I have the puppies, who I think are growing bigger daily, and I'm fine with that for now." Jenson called him a fool. "Perhaps I am, but like I said, I'm not going to rush into anything at the moment. Besides, she'd have to love dogs, as I'm not going to be getting rid of them. I love the little suckers."

"Sap." The next house was something along the size of his parents' home. The one that they took after giving Clay the manor home. Getting out of the car to have a look around, he was dismayed to find that the snow they'd had last night hadn't done a thing in hiding the work that needed to be done to the yard. It was not just overgrown with weeds about two feet tall, but there were things in the yard, things he didn't have names for, that made him think of a haunted house rather than one that he wanted to spend his golden years in. "This is all the yard that you get. Right in front of the house. I don't know what I'd do if I didn't have a nice big yard around my house with the pool."

"You're right about the yard. I don't think that I'd even want this place if it was perfect inside without a back yard. And the front one is in need of too much work to consider buying it."

They moved on after about ten minutes of trying to get to the front porch. There weren't any more homes on his list, and he was really disappointed in the realtor on that, but they saw several for sale signs, and they didn't feel cheated out of what they'd seen. They stopped at the next house on a whim. As soon as they cleared the trees in the front yard, Jenson whistled. This was a forever home, just not for him, he told his brother.

There were two people in the yard when they pulled up the drive. They were shoveling the driveway and talking. Asking them if they wanted to see the house, Trevor was almost afraid to see it. If he fell in love with it, he was going to forever blame Jenson as he told the couple that they'd love to see the house.

"I know you. You're...let me think. That's it. You're my congressman." Jenson shook hands with the couple and told them that he was still getting used to his new title. "I bet you are. I saw your wife in town a couple of days ago. My goodness, that little boy of yours sure does take after you, doesn't he?"

"He looks more like his mom, I think. But thank you for thinking that. No one notices me when they're around." They all laughed and Trevor shook their hands next. "My brother is looking for himself a forever home. He's got himself a couple of puppies that he's looking for a nice big yard too."

As soon as they got into the house, his brother took over talking to the couple and he made his way around the house. Christ, it needed nothing done to it as far as he could see. It was perfect. But for him? He still wasn't sure. He made his way to the back of the house through the kitchen. It, too, looked perfect to his eyes, and he saw the back yard.

Going out of the house and onto the large deck devoid of furniture this time of year, he looked at the expanse of the yard. He could raise all ten of the puppies that Gracie had found and not have to worry about them being overcrowded. There were trees in the fenced-in yard, three down the middle and four on each side, that gave the yard a very nice, shaded area. The couple, he'd never caught their name, had had a garden back there that looked like it had done well for them. There were still three large pumpkins in the place that he could see sitting on the wrap-around porch for the holidays.

Going back into the house, Trevor looked for flaws in his...the home. As far as he could see, it was ready to move in without so much as a dusting to make it better. He wanted to tell the couple to leave so that he could have it to sleep in tonight. But he'd learned from going to auctions that you never showed your hand when dealing with sales. He found them in the living room, with Jenson asking them questions about what they thought needed improvements in the town.

"Did you find the yard to your liking, Mr. Strong?" He asked them to call him Trevor. "All right. I know that the back yard is a bit much, but I'm betting that you'll find a way to fill it out with those puppies you have."

He had to bite his lip so that he'd not beg them to let him move in as soon as this afternoon. Sitting with the couple, he asked questions about the house. He thought he was doing well until their doorbell rang and it was another person wanting to see the house. Trevor looked at his brother.

"Calm down." He nodded and asked him what he was supposed to do. "Nothing. If you'd like, I can talk to them for you. You look like you've had the best Christmas, birthday, and any other holiday all rolled into one. I'll help you out with this. But you have to have Christmas here for the family. This place just screams family get-togethers for any reason."

When the couple came back, asking them if they had any more questions, it was when he asked the price. It was much bigger than he thought but he swore to himself it wasn't because he was a Strong. He wanted to tell them that he'd pay any price so long as he could have it.

It was Jenson that made the offer. He wanted to smack him around, telling him that he wanted the house bad enough to pay the asking price, but he seemed to know what he was doing. He was going to murder his brother or at least do him bodily harm if he lost this house. Leaning back on the couch he'd been sitting on. He closed his mind off to the conversation and thought about the investments he'd made just this morning on a large business that was going to bring several hundred jobs to the area. Not to mention, they were going to use local to build the plant. It wasn't until his brother poked him that he let go of his thoughts.

"We're leaving." He nodded at his brother, standing up when he did. "I've helped you out by making an offer on the house, and they want to see what this couple wants to do. I'd say that you're in for some bidding wars because they want to make it their family home, and it's just you. Not that that should matter, but I just have a feeling."

"Did you make an offer?" He said that he'd said he'd pay the asking price. "Good. This is a great house, don't you think?"

"I do. You zoned out there for a moment, and I told them that you were looking to expand jobs in the area and that you were thinking of what needed to be done to make it happen. It was sort of embarrassing when I think about it. What the hell were you thinking about?" He told him it was just what he'd said. "Oh. You have someone that wants to start up a business around here? That's awesome, little brother. I'm proud of you."

They were nearly to the car when the other couple came out of the house. Once they were gone, taking their time in getting the car started, he was both excited and nervous when the home owners came out to the car. They told them that the couple thought that the house was a little too big for them. Jenson said that the offer still stood if they wanted to think about it. They left soon after that.

He only then just realized that he'd only looked at the main level of the house and the yard and was sold on it. Trevor decided to ask his brother about the house. Since Jenson was driving now, he simply handed him a sheath of papers about the house.

"Eight bedrooms? It didn't look that big

for that amount of bedrooms." He explained that there were two bedrooms over the garage that also had a dinette set as well as a bath and living room. "That's kinda nice. I could have someone over if I wanted."

"You want the house then?" He said that he did and thought that the house was perfect the way that it sat. "I have to agree with you there. It also has a new furnace and air conditioner. The kitchen has been updated in the last year. There aren't any carpets in the place. That is something that Jade wanted in our new home, too. I like the hardwood floors and the way they feel when you walk around on them."

"What else can you tell me?" Jenson told him that the house had hardwood floors throughout. That, as he'd said, the furnace and the air conditioner had been replaced, the roof was new, and that the garage, while a new addition, had been made in the way of the house so that it blended in well. There were also fifty acres to the house that was used by the local farmers as an added income. "When did they say they'd get back to us? I'm assuming that you gave them your card."

"I put your number on the back so that they

can call you directly." He thanked his brother. "You owe me dinner. And if you get the house, you're going to babysit for Jade and me so we can have a nice dinner."

"Deal. Don't be surprised if your son loves me more than you guys when you get back." His brother told him that he thought that he could handle that. "You say that now, but you don't know what I have planned for the two of us when he comes over."

~*~

Debra was asked once again to come to the living room. She hated that room most of all. People were so nice and happy there and all she wanted to do was just be left alone so that she could think. And plan. They were even making that hard for her. Thinking and planning were what she did best.

Sitting on the couch as far away from the little shitter — their baby, she hated it when it would come up to the couch and make its way to her. It wasn't walking yet, but it did annoy her to the point that she wanted to go and get a butcher knife and cut off his head. The little monster would suck on his hands then touch her — Christ oh mighty, it would touch her with its grubby little hands.

"Does someone your age trick or treat?" She

asked what that was, knowing full well what it was and how it was supposed to end. She wanted to have to sacrifice something to the gods worse than she wanted these people to leave her alone. "If you want to, you can dress up in a way that would keep you from being recognized while out getting candy."

Jenson was an idiot, but Jade wasn't. Neither was Jenson, now that she thought about it. He was just a sap, what his brothers called him. Jade was sharp, and the way that she stared at her all the time, never leaving her alone in the house, especially around the baby, had her thinking that she could get into her head. She watched her like Mrs. J did toward the end of her life.

Her planning could only get her so far in what she wanted out of life. It was simple, really, her plan but not being able to get out and get it done, now that was a different matter altogether. She looked at Jade when she said her name. That was another thing that she wanted to get away from and that was to have people stop staring at her all the time.

"I asked you if you wanted to go trick or treating." Her voice had a tone to it, but she didn't know what she'd missed. Telling the woman that she didn't want to go or to dress up seemed to satisfy her. Screaming in her head, she smiled, knowing full well that it didn't even come close to looking like a smile but more of a grimace. Whatever. They were holding her back.

"How old are you? I've heard two different ages. I would have thought that your guardian would have been able to tell us the true age as she raised you from infancy." She stared at Jenson, wondering when he got so smart. Instead of answering him, Debra stood up and said she needed to go to the bathroom. "All right, Debra, if that's your real name, we'll pick up from there when you return."

"What's that supposed to mean?" Jenson shrugged, but she could tell that he was ready to get something more than she wanted to share. "I'm tired. I think I'll take—"

"The FBI is looking for you. I have a feeling that you even know what they're looking for you for." She sat down on the couch again and stared at him with her mouth open. "The only thing is, they don't call you Debra Carter but Lavender. Lavender Hunt. I know that it's you because they told me about the scar that you have on your left shoulder. It's from when you were shot six months ago when they had you trapped, or so they thought, while you were robbing a bank. You're very enterprising for someone who claims to be only eight years old. Not that I don't think an eight-year-old could have some skills, I think, and this just could be me, but I think that you're closer to the twelve-year-old that they say you are." She laughed. It was about as forced as she could make it.

"I just don't know what you're talking about. I mean, the FBI? What could they want with me?" He told her. "Murder? Attempted murder too? Why, I'm just a kid."

"Sure you are." The front doorbell rang and she was frightened when she couldn't go and hide. Jenson told her to have a seat still and that these people wanted to talk to her. "They have a few questions to ask you and are, for their own reasons, I guess, going to take you in. That's who you've been hiding from, isn't it? I mean, you had Mrs. J. fooled into thinking that it was some bad guys that wanted you but it's really nothing more than the Feds as well as a few other departments with initials on their flak jackets."

"You'll not do this to me." It was Jade who asked what she was going to do about it if they didn't turn her over. "I'll kill you all. I know how, too."

"So do I." The men came into the room just as Jade pulled her gun. "I'd like to say that this has been fun, but really, it's not been. You're a monster. And I'm glad to have you out of m—"

"Mommy, you can't do this to me. I'm just a little girl?" It had worked before for her, whining to Mrs. J when things weren't going her way. Mostly, it was that she needed money for something, school supplies, she told her, but really, she'd been hiding guns all over the other house just so she could never be caught like she was right now. She turned to Jenson. "Please? Daddy, I don't want to go with them. They'll hurt me, take me apart like I'm something of a monster, and all I wanted to do was to stay alive."

"You're not going to win any favors by using that tone with me. I've been reading over the file of Lavender Hunt for a few days now." She stood up and reached for her gun. When she couldn't find it, she began looking for it in the cushions of the couch. It was one of the men that their butler let in that laughed.

"Hello, Lavender. It's been a long time in coming." She said that she didn't want to go and that they'd made a mistake. "As much as I'd love to tell you that we never make mistakes, I can tell you right now that we haven't on you. Your gun is the one pointed at you. Jade and her husband have been pretty good at keeping an eye on you for us."

She wanted to run and turned to do so, but she felt the first bullet hit her in the back. Before she fell fully to the floor, two more shocking pains took her breath away. Unable to feel her legs, she tried crawling to the patio doors. They'd kill her if they caught her, and that just wasn't in the books for her. Before she got more than a foot from the door, someone put their booted foot on her shoulders.

"Damn you, you mother fuckers. What the hell is this all about?" The man closest to her said it was about the nineteen deaths that she had been a part of. "I'm a kid."

"Yeah? Well, it didn't seem to matter when you and your gang were robbing homes, only to end up killing off the homeowners. We know how you got into the house by pretending to be a long-lost child and preying on their hearts." She struggled to get away, but she wasn't moving. "We've been able to catch your gang, too. They didn't particularly like working for you. They said you were meaner than a rattlesnake when you were pissed off. Each of them is singing to the heavens about all the shit that the five of you have been doing."

"Which one of them told on me?" she was told that once they had them in a cell, they were happy to talk about her. "I knew I couldn't trust them. But it's difficult to find good help when you need it. Damn it all to fuck and back. I almost had the most killed for my age. Just two more—if you didn't count school shootings. Christ, you couldn't just wait a few more weeks to turn me in, could you? You're lucky that your brat isn't counted in the dead. I hate that little fucker more than I do you two."

She was read her rights four times before they put her in a van. Each department made sure they were able to get their piece of her, too, by frisking her over and over. The mother fuckers even took her boots off that she'd worked a week on to have a blade put into the top of them. She supposed she had the Strongs to thank for them finding it so quickly. The sides of the van were reinforced steel bars and a long bench in the back that they chained her like a dog, too. She saw Jade standing on the patio when she was finally locked in.

"I'll be back. No one will want to convict me once I have my day in court. I'll make sure they see me as this little kid who doesn't understand what they're doing to me." Jade laughed, threw back her head, and laughed hard. "What do you find so funny now? Just so you know, as soon as I'm out, I'm coming after you and this pitiful family of yours."

"You're not getting a trial." She asked her what she was talking about. "Yes, you see, I told them just what you said to me, that a jury would be a waste of time. That's why they're taking you to a prison where you won't ever see another inmate or jailer but the ones that bring you your food. You won't even get any outside time like criminals do. That way, you will never be tempting anyone for so long as you live."

"You bitch. Everyone deserves a trial. You'll see." But she was beginning to worry now. None of the men were talking to her. They were…she wondered if the laughter she was hearing had to do with what the fucking bitch was saying. She asked the man who seemed to be the most in charge. He smiled at her, and she could see that he truly was enjoying whatever he had up his sleeve concerning her.

"You'll be remanded over to a maximum security prison. There will be no trial, and thanks to us finding your books, the ones that you didn't share with the Strongs, we'll have a wonderful time closing some cases that I'm betting you were in charge of. The murder of the nineteen people, three bank robberies, as well as the attempted murder of Mrs. J and the Strongs. Did you notice that they never drank whatever you brought to them in the name of thanking them for keeping you safe? Yes, ma'am, you're going to rot in jail, and there will be no one to mourn your death, nor care that you'll spend all your time alone without a single thing to distract you.

She was still yelling at them when the door to the van closed, and someone put a ball and chain over her mouth. There were four men in the sucker with her, and she couldn't talk to them. They'd put the gag over her mouth while each of the men had their guns pointed right at her. This was so not fair that she wanted to smack someone around. They didn't even care when she glared at them, the mother fucking assholes.

The ride was bumpy and twice she fell over. The first time, she got herself up, but the second time, she just laid flopped over. Bumping her head several times didn't seem to bother anyone but her and she was screaming at them around the ball. Christ, when she was set free, she was going to murder each and every one of them.

The van started to slow, and she wondered what was going on. There were no windows in front of her, so she wasn't sure what was going happening. The front of the van, where the driver was, didn't show her anything either, so she had to wait. Another thing that she hated to do was to wait on shit. She really was going to make each and every person suffer when she was freed.

Lavender didn't think that she'd be put in a real prison. She really was just a kid in age, but she'd been doing crimes for as long as she could remember. The only reason that Mrs. J was still alive was because she was a good cover for her. So long as she'd been in bed before the old bat got up, she was none the wiser. Or so she had thought. Apparently, she'd been keeping tabs on her as well. There wasn't enough trust in the world, she thought. Not even for a twelve-year-old girl who were trying to make the best out of her life.

Once the van stopped, again she fell over. She was pulled out by her chains. They never took their guns off her chest and head, and if the situation wasn't so serious, she might have laughed. An angel. That's all she needed was an angel that would get her out of this. Then she got a good look at the place where they'd taken her.

It was a jail, she supposed, but it looked more like concrete slabs stitched together to make the walls and roof. There were several of these… houses? Cells? She didn't know, but if they thought that she was going to be staying out here in the middle of nowhere with just four walls of gray concrete, then they were in for a big surprise.

"From now on, you'll be known as cellmate nine. For the rest of your life, you will be living… habiting in building number nine. There will be no contact with anyone. You'll have three meals a day every day that you're alive. There is no mail service out here, no internet nor will you be allowed anything other than what you need to keep you alive. If you die? You'll be buried in the fields beyond here without a marker or anything other to mark your passing but a slash on the building you died in to know that it's now empty and awaiting the next person who will live out their life. Do you have any questions?" She asked what she was going to get to entertain her, books or something. "Nothing. You'll need to figure out what you need on your own to keep you entertained. No one will give two shits if you're bored or not."

Shoving her into the building, she heard something slapping along the sides of the door. The man on the other side told her that he was sealing her into her dwelling so that she'd not get out. They actually concreted her into the building so that she'd not be able to get out. The only opening that she had was the opening over the far door that she knew was going to be for her food to come in.

She was never going to make it in here. Surely, they were kidding about her being stuck in this place and expected to live out the rest of her life. Christ, she realized, she might live for another seventy or so years like this.

Sliding down the wall, not hearing a thing going on around her, Lavender thought perhaps she was well and truly caught this time. Feeling the tears fall down her face, she had a thought that this was what they were all laughing about. How a twelve year old was going to be living this way forever. Christ, she just wanted to start her life over.

Chapter 2

Trevor was reading over the paperwork that they'd gotten when Debra/Lavender had been taken away. It didn't seem so bad, only reading how she was going to be jailed, but when you had an active imagination like he did, he could see all kinds of horrors awaiting the child. No matter what she'd done, he couldn't think of her as anything other than a small kid who had gotten herself in trouble. Jade snorted when he said as much to her.

"Do you know how she killed her victims? Any idea what she had put the family through before they finally died from their extensive wounds?" He said he'd only read what he'd seen in the paper for her. "Yes, well, they watered it down a great deal. The public outrage would have been more than anyone would have been able to stomach."

"Because she was a child?" Jade told him that it was because she was a monster. "I'm sorry, but how does a kid know how to be a monster? I mean, she was literally a child living with a ninety-year-old woman. How did she get around that even?"

"She would, along with the two men that she had near her at the time would, sneak into the homes and do the damage then. But with a family back when she was ten, she went back there for three nights in a row to do what she did to them." Jade asked him if he thought he could handle it.

"When you put it that way, no, I don't know that I want to know. I'm curious, I'll tell you that, but I'm also afraid since you're calling her a monster. What did she do?" She asked him again if he was sure that he wanted to know. "I believe I do. So that I can get the image out of my mind on what she did as to what she actually did."

"The Palmer family was a family of five. Three children and the parents. They were well-to-do church-going people that were well-liked in the community that they lived in." He said that he'd read that. "What you won't read is how she killed them. The children were let off easy, in comparison. Their ages were ten, the same age as Lavender, eight and four—two boys and the youngest a girl. She killed them by hammering a nail into their temple. Not with a nail gun, but she actually hammered the nails into their heads while what we think the others watched on. After killing them, she put them into their rooms, not even in their beds, but just tossed them inside the room and didn't bother them again. But not the parents." He asked if this was far worse. "The woman died last, but while the man was alive, she played with them both. The man had several nails in his body, from his head to his toes. The nails were hammered in, and he was alive during this time. While still alive, she flayed his skin off his body. It must have been something new to her, but the first slices were clumsy and too thick. As she did more to his body, starting with his back, she got better at it. Seemingly, practice makes perfect. Also, his penis was missing. That's important."

Trevor started to make a joke, but it froze in his throat. The thought of someone having their dick taken off made his own cock hurt. Adjusting himself, he continued to listen to Jade as she seemed to be reliving the horrors of the house.

"He was found hanging from the upper floors. As soon as the front door was breached, the police ran into him, causing several of the seasoned officers to be sick. He'd been hanging there for several days before anyone noticed that they weren't doing their usual things like church and office." She looked out the window, no longer looking in his direction as she continued her tale. "The Feds were called in, and that's when I had a front-row seat to what she'd done. All I can say for sure about what I'm about to tell you is that putting her in the type of jail cell that she's in frightens me because of my fear of her getting out and continuing on her way to perfect her ways of killing. Then there was the mother. Christ, when I think about what she had gone through, it makes me sick again. The woman did suffer. There is no doubt about that. She would nearly kill her, back off a bit, then do more to her." She glanced at him before saying anything else. "She took a long rebar piece of metal and, again, pounded into her head. We're assuming it was her head first because she didn't fight her much after it was through her head. The rebar then went down along her spine, through her neck to her bottom. It came out of her rectum and then…and then she bent her feet in a way that made it so that the rebar was through her feet. All of this was in order to put her on a spit and roast her." She looked at him. "Her arms were chained to her body like someone would do a turkey. Her knees had been sewn together with the same chain that was around her arms. The man's penis was found during autopsy inside her vagina, then sewn shut. Christ. For four days, the woman was put on this thing and rolled — "

"Enough. I get the picture." He stood up, pulling Jade into his arms, and held her while she sobbed. It hurt him to his very core that this had hurt someone like his sister-in-law like it did. And he would bet that this would be a part of her nightmares for the rest of her life, too. "I'm so sorry that I was flippant about Lavender. I'm truly sorry that I made you relive it again, too. I love you, Jade."

Jade cried for twenty minutes or so. He continued to hold her even after Jenson, her husband, and his brother came into the house to find her. After he walked away, nodding once as if he understood what was going on, Jade pulled away and looked up at him.

"Her age is important to her being locked away because she will only perfect her ways of killing as she gets stronger. And she was nearly there now. We might never have been able to figure out that she killed those people if not for the fact that there was a single fingerprint in the blood on the body of one of the children. We all feared that as she got older, she'd be better at not leaving a trace behind, and we'd be looking for her all over the world."

"I'm sorry." She nodded and laid her head on his chest. "Whatever is being done to her, it's not nearly enough." Jade agreed with him. "I've been looking over the specs on the place that she is now. They're certainly not taking any chances of her getting out, are they? I mean, they concreted her into her cell so that she won't be able to bribe her way out of there. I had a thought that she was going to freeze to death in the winter but she won't, will she? She'll simply live because they want her to die."

Going back to his condo, he realized that he'd missed several calls. Listening to his messages as he walked back, he heard from the bank to see if he had applied for a loan through one of their branches and several calls from the realtor to ask him if he wanted to see any other houses. He'd not yet heard back from the couple selling their home, and he was getting nervous about that.

Stomping the snow off his boots when he got home, he looked around the condo and laughed. He'd been packing since he'd put a bid on the house, and it caused him to have to search the boxes for things when he needed them. In his mind, he wanted to be ready. It was his brother Maverick that suggested that he slow down. The couple had thirty days or more to move out. Of course, he had to tease him a bit, too, for jumping the gun.

Deleting all the other messages, it was just spam, he called the relator to ask if she had any houses to show him that weren't small. Of course, she told him, she had more larger houses that people didn't want any more than she did smaller ones. He didn't care to be cramped up in a house anymore. Taking the dogs out so they could do their business, he heard from the couple about the house. He'd gotten the house. Then, he was asked if they could have the next two weeks to move out. Trevor told them they could, thinking it was better than he'd thought, and told them that he was going to need that time to get things to fill out the house.

"We're going to auction off the things in the house that we're not taking. Would you like to come by and see what you might want to purchase? It's entirely up to you, but the house has more bedrooms than what we're going to be moving into, so we aren't taking any of them with us. Just the master suite of things." He asked how they would be pricing things. "The auctioneer told us that he could maybe get a few people gathered up, and we'd do it right in the rooms. It will all be sold at the same time per room. We just want out of this big house and move into something smaller on our daughter's land."

"I'd love that. And if I win the bid, it will be one less thing that I have to worry about getting." He was almost giddy with the prospect of getting his house laid out so soon. Of course, he'd never seen the bedrooms, being too excited to get the house when he'd been there, but he thought that if he didn't like it, he'd just not bid. Or perhaps bid low with the hopes of getting them cheaper and replacing them as he found things that he liked. "You tell me when you're going to do it, and I'll be there. I love this idea. Thank you."

"We're just so happy to be getting into something smaller, young man, because we're not as young as we used to be, and stairs are killers. The deciding factor was when my wife fell down them, breaking her wrist and foot. No more stairs for us, we decided." Trevor told him how sorry he was to hear that. "You've no idea what it was like to find your wife lying on the floor sobbing about how she hit her head on the floor and her wrist and foot hurt badly."

He said that he'd call him back when he had a date and time. Trevor did a little dance in the snow when he closed the connection. The puppies were having such a good time in the yards that he had a hard time wrestling them into listening to him. Taking the dogs back in the condo, he knew that the dogs were going to love the fenced-in back yard, too.

Getting online when he got back in his place, he looked for prices on bedroom sets. He wasn't really sure what was in the rooms. Were there two dressers or one? Did they have nightstands or not? So to get himself a good pricing, he wrote down what he thought it might well cost for the entire room full of things for himself. Also, what he thought individual prices might be on each item. It was a great deal more expensive than he realized. Even putting in the cost of wear and tear on things.

Making dinner for himself, he played with the dogs. They really were a great source of entertainment, but they were also very messy what with knocking things over and slobbering on everything. He couldn't wait until they were bigger so that he could get them to settle down. However, watching some people's dogs in the complex, he did wonder what he'd gotten himself into by taking two dogs instead of just the one. Smiling to himself, he knew that everyone had taken a couple of the pups, so he wasn't too worried yet. He might even send them off to training school to have them behave when he wasn't around.

At about half past six, the Courtrights called back. There was going to be an auction in the morning. They wanted it finished with what they had to move out as yet and that there would be three more groups there. He was happy about that but also going to take his dad with him. Or his mom. She'd glare at the other groups if they outbid him, and he'd win that way. He wasn't his mommy's baby for nothing.

It just so happened that his mom was busy with her tea club—he didn't understand why they called it that, rarely did they ever drink tea—but his dad was free. Going to bed that night, he wasn't sure if he was going to be able to sleep as his excitement level was through the roof. Christ, he was about as excited as he'd been as a kid when Christmas and his birthday rolled around.

~*~

Henrie wasn't sure why she'd been asked to drive her truck to the address that was on the paperwork.

Sure, it was a big house, and she knew that things needed to be moved out, but she wasn't going to lift anything, nor was she going to assist in it either.

There were rules with her company and one of them was you do not get involved with moving things that are not a part of her company. Like the company she worked for delivered couches to stores all over the state of Ohio and West Virginia, but she only had to back her rig up to the distribution center, and they did all the lifting.

Having to take her rig to a person's house without being told there would be help made her nervous about what was going to happen. After parking in the long U-shaped drive, she got out and went to find a Mr. Peabody and ask about why she was there. At so fucking early in the morning too.

Finding the owners of the house, they were confused as well as to why she was there, the man told her where to find Mr. Peabody. This was costing him nearly four hundred bucks an hour, according to the sheet she'd been given. She hoped that this wasn't going to be an all-day move. She had to work at ten tomorrow, taking a load to West Virginia. Peabody was standing in the hall next to what appeared to be a bedroom.

"There you are. You're late." She told him that she was on time, she didn't expect to have to walk around for forty minutes in trying to find him. "Well, you'd better be on standby in the event that I win the bids. I have to have things moved out as soon as I win them."

"I'm assuming that you have loaders." He asked her what she was talking about and Henrie knew this was going to happen and stretched her neck until it popped twice. "I don't load my rig. That's on you. I drive to and from, but that's the extent of my contract with you."

"No, I asked for someone to come and pick up the loads for me. That would be you. I hope you're stronger than you look because this is some heavy shit that they're selling. And I plan on buying it all." She pulled out a copy, not the original work that he had signed. "See right there, it says that you're going to be picking up loads that I purchase."

"Picking up loads, I'm not going to be loading it. That's on you to take care of." He was shaking his head even as she pulled out her cell. After telling the dispatcher what was going on, she was told to hand the phone over to him. While he argued with her dispatcher, she decided to have a look around. It was a beautiful home, and she could only dream about living in something like this.

The first bedroom that she looked in had her whistling at the pieces. They were huge, but she could tell that they weren't any of that plywood stuff but solid wood, more than likely oak. Even the sleigh bed, being about a king, she would guess, would weigh more than five hundred pounds by itself. That wasn't even including the mattress that went with it. Smiling at the couple that was in the room when they smiled at her, Henrie backed out of the room to find that Peabody was still on the phone with her company—him getting louder all the time. She went into the second bedroom and then on to the third. That was where she fell in love.

The room was done up in earth tones. Browns, blues, and rusty reds that made her want to live out the rest of her life in here. The bed, another sleigh bed, seemed to be about the same size, but this room had end tables on either side of the bed as well as two large dressers that looked to be made of the same wood. Something like a dark chocolate did when she splurged on it. There was also a full-length mirror of the same wood that took up an entire corner of the room. She'd bet anything that the prices of these pieces would be around five grand total, if not more. And the man who had made arrangements to have her pick up the stuff didn't look as if he could afford one room, much less the six that was up on this floor.

"The two rooms over the garage have been emptied, so we don't have to go over there." The younger man who joined the well-dressed couple started talking as soon as they entered the room. "They've been broken down already and are in the garage. That's where they've been storing boxes as they load them up." She wondered if they had movers to load up their moving truck or not. She came into the hall just as Peabody was screaming at someone on the phone.

His face was red and ruddy looking. She knew the auctioneer as she'd been to several of his auctions before. The man was trying in vain to calm the man down. When Peabody tossed her phone at her, she barely caught it out of the air. Donna, the dispatcher, was still talking when she put it up to her ear to see what was going on.

"It's me." Donna told her to hang on a moment until she calmed herself down. When she let out several long breaths and counted to ten three times, she seemed to have a better control over herself. "Are you all right?"

"No. Good lord, Henrie, how is he talking to you?" She said that he'd walked away before speaking to her. "Well, don't you dare try and load that stuff up on your own. He didn't pay for loaders, and I'm not going to be messing with him anymore. Just drive. That's all you were hired to do."

"I told him that. That's why I called in rather than to argue with him. Though I have to admit, he does seem to like the sound of his own—" The couple with the younger man came to ask her something. Telling Donna that she'd call her back, she put the phone in her pocket. "Yes, what can I do for you?"

"He's showing off." The woman leaned in and whispered her observation. "The man was just saying to the auctioneer that he wasn't going to have you take anything. He was just trying to intimidate anyone who tried to bid against him. That he was so sure that he was going to win the bids that he hired you to come here and pretend."

"I hope he realizes that I'm not pretending with him. The company I work for is getting four hundred bucks an hour, and they're not messing around." The woman laughed. "I'm Henrie Banister. I work for Banister and Banister Drivers."

"My name is Lisa, and this is my husband, Barkley. Our son, the man who bought this house is Trevor. He was invited here to see if he wanted the furniture that was in the rooms so that they didn't have to be moved. I do believe this furniture isn't going to go cheaply, do you?" She told her that she didn't know much about wood or furniture that was made from it. Her firm only delivered it to stores. "What a lovely job. Do you get to see much of the country?"

"No, ma'am. Just a couple of states." She tried to back away, but she pulled her right to her to continue talking. It was a little disconcerting to be talking to a stranger about what she did for a living. "I've been riding and driving since I was twelve. You have to be twenty-one to drive a big rig."

"Oh, Banister. I know that place. We've used them a few times when we wanted something moved. Very good company. Are you related to them?" She told her that they were her grandparents and parents. "Oh, how lovely. Did you hear that, Trevor? She works for her family, too. I love it when a family can pull together and be a part of something larger. Good for you. Trevor, this is Henrie Banister." She went on to tell him how she was related to them.

"I should be getting back to my rig, Mrs. Strong." She wasn't given a last name, but she knew who they were. Instead of releasing her arm, she took her hand into hers, telling her she might as well watch the show as she thought it was going to be fun. "All right, I suppose. I can stay for a few minutes."

Henrie knew on some level that she wasn't going to be leaving her side until the entire show, as she called it, was over. Staying out of the way, she was dismayed to find that she was standing very close to Trevor when he turned and winked at her.

"My mom is playing matchmaker." She sputtered at him. "Don't worry. I'm on to her. I'm assuming that you're single?"

"Yes. But I have no desire to be matchmade with anyone." He said he didn't either. He just wanted to fill his house out. "Well, good luck with that. I think I'll go to the truck."

"Don't. Please. She'll just find someone else to introduce me to, and I'd rather just be able to focus on the bidding." She nodded, not at all sure why she was giving in so easily.

When the auctioneer started telling the rules of the day, Peabody pointed out that she was there to load the things that he bought, all the furniture into her rig right away. Before she could tell him again that she wasn't, he looked at her like he'd murder her if she said a word to the contrary. She didn't think that anyone in their right mind thought that she could lift even the mattress off the beds much less the entire rooms full of furniture. It was, as Mrs. Strong said, a scare tactic so he could intimidate the other bidders.

The bidding always started out incredibly high. Although she didn't think that ten grand was a bad price for the stuff in the first room. When it got down to five hundred, the bidding began.

Trevor won the first room. It had been close, and Peabody was pissed off. Henrie was so excited for Trevor that she hugged him. Embarrassed now, he smiled at her, and she could see why the entire world was waiting with bated breath for the last Strong man to get married or at least find himself a wife.

He was charming and beautiful. Men she knew were supposed to be handsome, but he was simply beautiful to her. His hair was a shade or two darker than his mother's, not including the little bit of gray that she had, and he had an air about him that made you think that he knew he was good-looking but just didn't care. She thought that was what everyone saw in good-looking men. Not her. She didn't want anything to do with charm and good looks. That had nearly ruined her mom and dad's life together.

Her dad had been out of the picture since she'd been about four. Her parents had married only to give her a last name. Mom had had enough and got her trucker's license and took to the road. Dad thought that, for whatever reason, he still could rule her mom. He found out the hard way that not only could he not rule either of them, but his looks never played into her mom's life with him. She thought that he'd been nice and that was as far as she went with him.

"Henrie?" She looked at Mr. Strong when he said her name. "We're moving to the next room, honey, and Trevor is telling his mother that you're his good luck charm. Are you coming?"

"He doesn't even know me." The older man laughed and said that Trevor was having fun with his mom, that she'd been going out of her way to see him married. "So long as she knows that I'm not the marrying type. I have just what I need now. Not some man that will be expecting me to—I'm going to shut up now. Yes, I'll go with you. But I'm not his charm or anything else of his."

Trevor won the next four rooms with only two more to go. Peabody wasn't being a good loser, going around and knocking against things that Trevor had won in the rooms. When they were on the last two, Mr. Courtright pulled him aside and asked to speak to him. Trevor grabbed her hand, pulling her along with them out into the hall and into one of the already purchased bedrooms.

"If you get the last two rooms, we'll give you the ones over the garage. We never expect to get as much as we have been. Thank you for that, but it's fun to see that other man get his nose bent out of joint about you winning. I told Sally that I'd almost make up the difference if you were to get to your limit and help you buy them anyway." He laughed. Wren, his name was said he'd not had this much fun in a very long time. "I swear to you, I'd sell off the rest of the house if I knew it was going to be this much fun."

Not only did Trevor win the last two rooms and get the other furniture, but Sally said that she was going to sell the dining room table as well.

They'd only just figured out that they weren't going to have room for it.

By the time the bidding was to begin on that for the house, Peabody was dressing her down for *cahooting* with the enemy. She didn't even know what that meant. She'd only been standing around until Trevor started holding her hand. As soon as the bidding war was over, she got into her rig to get the paperwork for the job today. And just as she thought that he'd do, Peabody said he wasn't paying as she hadn't done a damned thing for him. Henrie called her grandda.

Chapter 3

Henry was having a hard time in keeping up with the conversation that Peabody was telling him about since he said that his employee had been *cahooting* with the enemy and holding hands with him. He knew a bit about the other people that were at the auction this morning but he also heard that his baby girl was hanging out with the Strong family. It was all he could do not to dance himself a jig while Peabody bitched at him about fairness and the price of four hundred dollars an hour for her doing nothing.

"You knew the price it was going to be before you had her showing up at seven in the morning to hang around and doing nothing. You were also told that she wasn't going to be loading a dammed thing for you, so you might as well get over that part. She's strong enough to do it, but I don't pay my drivers to be lifting heavy things when they don't have to. I know too that Donna told you several times — we have it recorded with you agreeing with my employee that you'd get your own people to load the...think how much money you saved in not having to hire loaders when you didn't win anything."

"He cheated." Henry laughed and asked him how Mr. Strong had cheated. "He had more money to spend than I did. Who pays a grand for a bedroom suit that is used? So what if it's solid oak? It's still used. I should have been able to get that stuff for five bucks a room. I tell you that even going to auctions is getting to be cutthroat nowadays."

Henry winked at his lovely wife, Anna, and put the phone on speaker so she could hear what the man was saying to him. He was glad that Henrie had given him a heads up on the man being mad when she'd gone home. But she hadn't said a word about holding hands with one of the Strong men.

When Peabody got belligerent, he hung up the phone. Since the man had put a credit card number down to rent the rig today, he went ahead and charged him the five hours and smiled while he was doing it. That would teach him to think that he could fool someone like him. He looked at Anna when the charge went through.

"What did he say?" Henry told her what had transpired before she'd come into the room. "He said he cheated because he had more money? Good heavens, Henry. What a thing to be upset about. Of course, he has money to spend. He has a good family that has been saving this town forever. Even he should understand that. But what of his story about our Henrie holding hands with one of the Strong men? I believe the only one that is left is the baby, Trevor. And I believe that he's in his mid-twenties."

"That's what I heard as well, that he was the baby. Wouldn't it be great if they were to hook up? However, that young man is in for a rude awakening if he thinks that she'll be easy. She's hard on men." Anna agreed reminding him of her boyfriend in high school. "Yes, he thought just because she was beautiful, she was stupid too. I doubt he's made that mistake again with any woman."

They both laughed thinking about the kid that had tried to take advantage of Henrie. He'd pretended to have car trouble and she'd gotten under the hood and found out that someone had pulled the plugs on his distributer. Once she fixed it, she made him get in the back seat, and she drove herself home. The kid had never lived it down what she'd had done to him, and he moved away. Best thing that had ever happened to Henrie. No one ever tried to take advantage of her again.

Henrie was coming to their house for dinner. He was sure that it was the only meal that she got that wasn't fast food. Her life had been doing one thing after another, and he didn't know what he'd do without her. She was his heart and soul next to his wonderful wife. He never regretted a day that they'd taken her in when she'd been ten years old.

She showed up just as they were having a nice chat in the living room. He didn't want to ask her about the Strong man because he didn't want to embarrass her. Apparently, his wife had no such trouble.

"Are you seeing Trevor?" He watched as her face turned a bright shade of pink and smiled to himself. Even if she said she wasn't, he could tell that she'd been thinking about him. "He's a good man, from what I hear. Comes from a good family, too."

"Are you tired of me and trying to get rid of me?" Anna tsked at her. "No, I'm not seeing him. He considered me his good luck charm or something, and he dragged me from room to room to get the rest of the household goods for the house he just bought. Did you know that the Courtrights are moving into a smaller home? I think that they mentioned that it was closer to their children. Now, there is a nice couple."

"Don't fob me off, young lady. Peabody told us that you were holding hands with him. You couldn't do better with him in your life." She told them that she wasn't looking for anyone to be in her life just now. "Still. He must have liked you well enough to have you in his court. Did you happen to know what he paid for the bedroom furnishings?"

"Not as much as I think they would have gone for. Most of the people there weren't bidding, but I think just having a look around. He got a good deal on the rooms. There isn't anything that he's going to have to do to move right in. They even sold the dining room table and chairs that they couldn't take with them."

They talked about the house that he had gotten and how perfect it seemed to be. She told them how the kitchen was up to date, a thing that would take the most time in remodeling, and now that he was outfitted with the bedrooms and dining room things, he could move right in like he'd been living there all his life.

"I've never been in their home. Not to say I'd not been invited but there was something always taking us away from going. I know that they used to throw the best Christmas parties when their kids were home. I'm glad that they're going to be moving closer to them. My goodness, they must be in their late seventies by now." Henry didn't point out that they were just hitting their mid-seventies this summer. That would put him in the dog house, and he loved being around his wife when she was just a little—a tiny bit—upset.

Dinner was great, but he thought that it was the company. He so loved cold meatloaf sammiches as a dinner and would eat his weight in them if he wasn't careful. Not really, but he would have the cook make the meatloaf the day before, the smell of it baking making his mouth water, and the next day they'd have their dinner. It was one of the few things that he enjoyed more than his wife. She liked them but not like he did.

After dinner, he watched as Henrie dozed off and on throughout the evening. He wanted to suggest that she just spend the night; there was plenty of room, but she'd leave, and he didn't want her to do that, being as obviously exhausted as she was. She finally dozed off into a deeper sleep, and lying her down on the sofa, he covered her up, and he and Anna went to their bed. It had been a long day, and he, for one, was ready for the next day. Just as he was lying down, it only being about nine o'clock, his cell phone rang. It was the service that he employed to answer the phone when the business was closed for the day.

"I have a Mr. Trevor Strong on the phone, sir. He wants to talk to you about your granddaughter." He asked her what he'd said. "He wants you to give her his phone number so that she can call him. Something about a good luck charm. I wouldn't have bothered you about it, but he's a Strong, sir, and I, for one, have trouble turning them down for anything."

"Yes, I know what you mean. All right, Hilda. Give him my house number and tell him that we were just off to bed. Ask him to come have breakfast with us in the morning and he can give it to her himself. She's staying the night here." He hoped that she'd be there in the morning and not take off in the middle of the night when she realized where she was. "Tell him that we eat at seven sharp and for him to wear his laze about clothing. I'm going to put him to work with...

never mind. Just do that for me, and we'll be set up."

When he put the phone down on his dresser, he couldn't help but dance. He'd been doing that for most of the day since he'd heard from Peabody, and he was having a wonderful time with knowing that maybe, just maybe, his wonderful granddaughter was going to be taken care of when he and Anna were no longer around. Christ, he loved his Henrie. She was the best thing that had ever happened to them.

She'd only been an infant when her parents were divorced. For whatever gods were watching over her that day, Henrie had been spared the fights between both her parents. There were times when he loved his daughter-in-law more than his own son. He'd messed up with Sharon, demanding that she hand over Henrie so that he could raise her on his own. He'd only wanted the child support that she'd give him if he won. They'd long since written him out of the will that would have made him millions of dollars. As it was now, Henrie was getting the bulk of their massive estate, and there was even money for Sharon. She had been a good person to all of them.

He couldn't sleep, not right now, so when

Anna turned off her light and rolled to her side, he got up. She wouldn't have woken if a bomb went off. She was such a heavy sleeper. Going to his office, he turned on his computer and did a search on Trevor Strong and the rest of the family.

My goodness, he thought the things that they'd done in their helping their town was a long list. And they didn't seem to be stopping anytime too soon. That's when he found out that Jenson Strong had been elected for their congressman, and he was glad that he'd made it. The boy was going to do good things even if he only did half of what he promised he'd do once he was in office.

Trevor was a good man. He had invested well with his brothers' help and had managed to save millions of dollars on his own. The family as a whole was worth billions and he decided right then and there he was going to have Maverick help him with some of his money. It was never too late to invest so that Henrie would have a better life than they'd had when they started out.

It was nearly three in the morning when he thought that he should go to bed. It didn't matter what time he would go to bed. He'd be up at six-thirty every day. He thought that was one of the things that he disliked about getting old.

Your body just seemed to have a mind of its own. Setting his alarm, just in case he did sleep over, he smiled to himself, thinking about the things that he'd been able to find out. While he'd been in his office, Henrie had awoken and he sent her off to be so that she'd not have to drive. He was surprised and pleased that she did just what he wanted. He didn't, however, mention that they'd be having company for breakfast in the morning. She'd leave for sure.

His alarm went off while he was reading the news on his phone. He was glad to see that Bradon Wallace had gotten life in prison plus one day. The judge must have been old school he'd not heard that saying in some time. Usually, it was life without parole. But it was good too for the Strong family to have the man in prison. He'd caused enough trouble for Gracie Strong, and a man didn't deserve it any better than he did. He told Anna about it when she got up.

"I read about him just the other day. Can you imagine stealing millions of dollars from his own niece? He wasn't even the person who should have been in charge of her, either. I just hope when we're gone, a long time from now, that no one takes advantage of Henrie. Not that I'd think she'd

let them, but you never know about slick people."
He told her that he thought that Henrie had a good
head on her shoulders and be damned the man that
tried anything with her. "True. I have so much to
do today, Henry. I just don't know where to start. I
think I'll start with having a good breakfast."

"We're having company. I nearly forgot."
He told her about the phone call that he'd gotten
last night and how he'd invited the young man to
have breakfast with them. "I know that Henrie is
still here. She got up about midnight, and I sent
her to her room. She looked exhausted even after
taking a nap on the sofa."

"She's working too hard. There is no reason
for her to keep driving. Even though Sharon has
finally retired, Henrie still works. I wish she'd
just become a — well, she'd never be a woman of
leisure, but it was a nice thought anyway. I so love
that girl." He said that he did as well.

When they got to the kitchen, not only was
Henrie there but Trevor had shown up as well. He
could tell that she was irritated, which he didn't
blame her. They'd gone behind her back and set
the two of them up. Trevor was talking about his
house and how he was going to be able to move
into it within the next couple of weeks.

"Why are you here again?" Anna told her that he was a guest of theirs and for her not to be rude. "I wasn't being rude. I think that's a good question. There is a rumor going around town that you've met your future wife and that you'd be off the market soon. What are you, a slab of meat? What kind of saying is that? Off the market? I don't have any desire to become a housewife, especially to a house that flipping big."

"I didn't ask you to be. I'd hire a lot of staff if it came to that." He laughed, and Henry couldn't help but join him. That got him a glare from both Anna and Henrie. "It is a large house. I thought when I started looking into having my own place that I wanted smaller. But I got the two mutts out there, and now I want them to have a big back yard."

There were two of the cutest puppies in the back yard when he got up to look. One was all black, and the other was a shade or two lighter. They were having a good time, chasing sticks that his butler was tossing for them, and Alan looked as if he was having a good time, too. He'd never seen such a big smile on his face before.

"They were abandoned, and my sister-in-law brought them to the vet. Ten of them falling all over each other like they couldn't get close enough to her. She was going to keep them all, but I convinced her to let me have two of them, and the rest of the family took a pair of them as well." Anna asked him if he'd gotten a good deal on the house. "Yes, better than I thought I would being that it was only on the market for a few days. It also saved me a bit of money because they were in a hurry to sell so they could move closer to their daughter. She's going to keep an eye on them from now on, I guess."

They talked about everything under the sun while they ate. The cook, Sue, had gone all out when she realized that she was going to be cooking for more than the two of them. There was so much food that he despaired of having a lot of leftovers, but Trevor seemed to understand the assignment and ate whatever was left when the rest of them were full. Henrie didn't back off either when it came to filling her belly. He thought that she was too thin anyway.

~*~

Trevor knew that Henrie was upset with him. He had sort of blindsided her into spending the day with him. He didn't know why she seemed to intrigue him but when she was spitting mad, as she was right now, he thought her to be the most beautiful woman in the world. Of course, he didn't say that to her. He wasn't that stupid.

"Why couldn't you have come here yourself then called later to get someone to move this crap for you?" He didn't have an answer to that but did tell her that she was his good luck charm. "You won't think that when I bash your head in for dragging me out here today."

The auction had been one that his parents went to every month. It was the first Saturday, and he was excited to be able to find things for his own home this time. There were several pieces that— she bumped into him hard and he turned to see what was the matter.

"That's Peabody over there, I think." He looked, happy for the heads up about the man. "He's going to cause trouble if I don't miss my bet. I wouldn't engage with him if you can help it. My grandda said that he has been trouble since he was a child. I don't think he's going to be happy with me either since they put the charge through on his credit card today for having me hang around the other place for him."

"I'll protect you." She snorted and asked him if she looked like she needed protecting from a blowhard like him. "Good point. Then you protect me. I'm delicate."

She snorted again, and he threw back his head in mirth. He was having a good time, and they'd not even started bidding yet. But they did keep their distance from Peabody. There was no point in ruining everyone's fun for the man.

Since this was indoors, there was no reason for coats. It wasn't all that warm inside even, but with all the people and excitement it was comfortable. And there were lots of household items too, things that he didn't have in his house like pictures on the walls—there were a lot of pictures and paintings there. Some tools that he thought would come in handy if he needed them for a leak or something. There were also things like a computer desk that looked similar to the filing cabinet that he had. Lots of little things that he wanted to pick out for his home. He hoped that he could convince Henrie to help him with that as well.

He didn't know why he was pursuing her. He liked her all right. She was beautiful and strong-willed. Today she was wearing a pair of leggings that showed off every muscle in her body along with the curve of her ass. But she was standoffish.

Like she'd rather be anywhere but with him. That didn't bother her either, as he was enjoying her honesty about being around him. Sometimes, it hurt, but for the most part, he laughed at her.

He saw her standing with his mom and wondered what they were up to. Then he saw the box of teacups in front of her, and they were talking about them. Mom used to collect teacups and saucers but she'd gotten tired of them taking up all the room she had them in and had sold them off. Someone had gotten quite a collection, he remembered, and his mom was happy with the room again. He thought that she had been gathering snowmen now. Not large ones, but some that, at the most, about as big as his hand. He noticed, too, that there was a box of those nearby as well. He came up behind them just as Peabody noticed that he was there.

"There you are. You gotta sell me one of those bedroom sets for you stealing them from me." He told the man no and felt the tension in Henrie as soon as he looked at her. "I gotta beef with you too. Your boss, he charged me for you sitting around on your ass at the auction yesterday morning when you helped him win all those rooms of furniture. I'm going to dispute the charge and we'll see what that gets that company."

"Yeah? Well, good luck with that. He also sent in the paperwork that you signed, stating that you were going to pay the money if you won anything or not. Also, I have it on good authority that it about overcharged your card that you left on file to pay for the privilege of having me around." He asked her why she thought it was a privilege. "Because without me there, you might well have won some of it. Then what would you have done with the furniture since I wasn't going to drag it out to the rig?"

"That's not right." She shrugged, and he looked at him. "You owe me at least one of the bedroom sets. I got a daughter moving back in with me and I need the extra beds."

"I don't care." He looked like he was going to hit him, with his fist doubled up and his arm tight. "I'd think very hard on your next move, Peabody. I'm not a little person, and I won't allow you to hurt or bully me. I'm a grown man about half your age and your weight. Don't mess with me."

"You think you're all that, do you? I'll have you know that I've had men like you hurting in ways that they never bothered me again." Trevor just stared at him and was glad when his dad and Barton showed up behind Peabody.

Trevor took a step back, but he didn't back down. Asking his mom and Henrie to please move away from him, he nearly took his eyes off of Peabody when they did. It was the move without argument that surprised him the most.

"Mr. Peabody, you might want to have a look around you before you do something that your bottom can't cover. My oldest is here, and he's got all kinds of people around him to protect his family. You make a wrong move and I'm sure that they'll have no trouble running you in for threatening this family. Again." Dad turned Peabody around so that he was facing him. "Don't do it. I'd hate very much for this place to become a crime scene. I love coming here with my family."

"You Strongs. You're all a bunch of pussies, as far as I can see. Standing behind some kind of hit squad when all I wanted to do was to have a conversation with your son here. He robbed me of some things the other day, and he should be made to pay up. You, being his father, you should know that he took advantage of a situation because he has more money than I do." Dad asked him what he was saying. "I could have had all that stuff if he wasn't rich. He should have given someone else a chance to get some of the goods. It's not fair that he can flaunt around his money when people are around."

"Are you saying that you're harassing my son and his girlfriend because he has more money than you do? That's the stupidest thing I've ever heard." Dad laughed, a short bark of laughter that didn't sound like he found anything funny. "There are a lot of people that have more money than we do. You don't see us complaining and causing trouble with them, do you? Get out of here before I use some of my considerable money and have you arrested. I will, too. Get away from us before...just get away before you bite off more than you can chew."

"I can chew plenty, so you know." Trevor was as confused as his dad looked. "Just leave me alone, the lot of you. Rich people like you shouldn't be allowed to mingle with people like us."

Whatever that meant, Trevor was all right with it. It made Peabody leave them alone and to walk away to the door. He hoped that he'd leave, but he had a feeling that he was going to regroup and come at them again. The bastard had taken a little fun out of his day, and he didn't—

The slap to his face startled him. Mom and Dad walked away with his brothers, but Henrie stayed. He asked her why she'd hit him. Before he allowed her to answer him, he pulled her into his arms and kissed her on the mouth. When he set her back from him, he thought that she was going to kill him where he stood.

"He had a gun." His lust-filled mind couldn't understand what she was talking about. When she drew back to hit him again, no doubt, he grabbed her fist this time and kissed it before putting it down at her side. "He was fingering his gun like he was going to shoot you with it. Didn't you see it?"

"No, I didn't." He waved at Jenson, and he came to him immediately. "Henrie said that Peabody has a gun on him. There is clearly a sign on the front door not to be having weapons on you when coming through the doors." Jenson told him that he'd take care of it and walked away. Trevor looked at Henrie. "I'm sorry."

"For what? For scaring ten years off my life? For fucking around with an unstable man? Or is it for not correcting your father when he called me your girlfriend? Any or all of those pissed me off." He asked her if she would be his girlfriend.

"No, I would not. You're not right in the head. You needlessly provoked that man, and it was stupid of you."

"I didn't know that he had a gun, not that that should make a difference. You're right. I shouldn't have provoked him into getting pissed off. I'm sorry." She still looked upset, and he ran his fingers down her cheek. "Your skin is just as soft as I thought it would be. And your lips taste like honey to me. Did you use something on them to lure me in to kiss you? I'll do it again if you don't mind."

"I do mind, you idiot." She turned on her heel and left him standing there. Just as he was thinking about how much fun it was to piss her off, he heard a gunshot. It was all he could do not to run into the scene when he counted the heads of his family and couldn't find Henrie.

Walking slowly, telling himself that she was going to be just fine; he was just coming to the woman down when Jade screamed at someone to call an ambulance. It was Henrie. She was done, and for the life of him he couldn't get his mind and body to work to see if she was all right.

"Trevor. Are you listening to me?" He nodded about all he could do now that things had started to come clear to him. "Trevor Strong. Look at me. Look. I'm fine."

Getting down on his knees, he took Henrie's hand into his. She must have said to him that she was fine another five times before Jade knocked him over. She told him that he was in the way and that they'd be able to get her to the hospital if he were to allow her to examine her.

"Yes, all right." He didn't let go of Henrie's hand but held it tightly in his own while Jade barked orders to the people around them. When his dad, he knew it was him by the heavy weight of his hands on his shoulders touched him, Trevor told his dad that Henrie was all right. "She's been shot, but Jade said she's going to be fine."

He hoped so. With all his heart, he hoped so. Even though she was talking to Jade and him, the pool of blood beneath her spread out. Once it touched his knees, he had to work hard at not freaking out. Then she told him that he needed to call her grandparents.

Chapter 4

Henry watched the young man pace. His entire family was with them, but he only had eyes for Trevor. When he'd called him a few hours ago, he'd been calm and collected. Since arriving at the hospital, he'd been anything but. He thought for sure one of his sisters-in-law was going to smack him around. Hearing what Jade had said to him before she'd gone into surgery with Henrie, he was sure that if she was out here, he'd be sitting in a corner with his thumb in his mouth. She was scary.

"It's taking longer than they said." He held onto Anna's hand and said that didn't mean anything, that they told them it would be two hours or more. "I know, but I want to see her. We didn't get to before they sent her off to surgery."

"Jade told us that she just needed to remove the bullet from her ribcage, and she'd heal from that. We need to not worry if there is nothing to worry about. She's going to be spitting mad when she finds out how many people are here for her. And to be honest with you, I'm glad for the company." She said that she was as well. "I know. They are very good at keeping people calm, don't you think?"

"Except for Trevor. He looks like he's about to explode." He had to agree with her and laughed a little. "I guess I didn't know that things had progressed that far between the two of them. He's worrying after her like she's his wife or something. And if he keeps pestering the nurses, they're going to sedate him and put him in a room alone."

He laughed, drawing attention to them. Waving off the Strongs, he was thrilled when one of the women, Carrie, sat a little girl in his lap. Her name was Sunny, she told him before she handed off one to Anna. Her name was Bethany. They were the cutest little girls he'd ever seen, and loved that they were dressed in similar but not matching dresses. Their little shoes, too, were something that he found amusing. Black patent leather shoes with lacy socks that had him thinking of his own granddaughter.

"Mr. & Mrs. Banister? I have some information on Henrie if you'd like to follow me." Anna said that they could talk in front of these people because they were there when she'd been hurt. "All right. The surgery is over. Doctor Strong said to tell you that Henrie is about as stubborn as she is. Also that Miss Henrie will have to stay in the hospital for a few days. The bullet broke three ribs when it entered her in the back."

"The man that shot her, can you tell me what's happened to him?" She said that she didn't have any information on him but would find out for them. "He shot her in the back. There has to be some rules about hurting someone when their back is turned."

"I'm looking into it, Mr. Banister." He nodded at Jenson and thanked him. "That's all right. Two men on my team were hurt as well, so that'll carry a heavy penalty for him."

It was nearly three hours later that they got to go to her room. They'd had her in intensive care for a while, making sure that her ribs were going to be all right. When he sat in the chair next to her bed and took her hand, he broke down in tears for the way that she looked lying there.

"She looks so tiny, don't you think? And pale. She's usually so brown this time of year when the winter months come along." Squeezing her hand, he was thrilled when he felt her squeeze it back. "I think she's waking up. I would love to have her complaining about all the fuss that is going on around her."

Trevor and his family stood around the room, but one by one, the others left them to her. Mr. Strong, Barkley, told him that he could contact him later. Just as Jenson was leaving, his cell phone rang and he went to the hall to answer it. When he came back in, he told them that Peabody was dead, that he'd tried to get away from the police when they were arresting him, and he didn't fare as well as Henrie. He told him, too, that it didn't end there. They were going to make sure that he paid even after death.

"My goodness, I've read about that." Anna spoke to Trevor when Jenson and the others had left. He tuned her out to watch his baby girl sleep. She was his world and he didn't mind saying that to anyone that came into the room with them. He half listened to Anna as she spoke to Trevor. "The courts will continue with a trial to make sure that any victims' families are taken care of. Yes, that's what it said, I just remembered that."

Wiping at the tears when Henrie looked at him, he asked her how she was feeling. Of course, she had to be a smart ass and tell him that she felt like she'd been shot. Holding onto her hand, he told her about Peabody too.

"He tried to kill Trevor. I heard him saying that the little bastard was right there, and I tried to wrestle the gun from him. He was going to kill someone over a couple of beds, grandda." He burst into tears again, just holding onto her hand. "I didn't even know he was that close to Trevor when I felt the burning of the shot. At first, I thought that I'd been just cut with a knife or something. What is wrong with people nowadays, grandda? I think I'm going to stay in my truck from now on and not interact with people."

"I don't know, baby, I don't know what most people are doing nowadays." He kissed the back of her hand. "Trevor is here with us. I'm going to leave you to him while I take your grandma down to get her something to eat. I don't want her to get sick when we're going to have to be taking care of you, love."

"I'll be fine. Tell him to go home." When she closed her eyes, he knew that she was still drugged up. Getting up, he told Trevor what she'd said, and he just knew that he was going to stay put. There was something about him that made him think he was going to be family, even if Henrie managed to push him away. He and Anna made their way to the cafeteria to get some much-needed food. He needed to eat because of his diabetes, and Anna, she needed to eat with him to make sure he was eating the right things.

The place was empty now. It was late, he realized, later than he'd even thought. But once they were seated with their trays, neither one of them could eat. Anna sobbed in her handkerchief, and he tried his best to be strong for her. It was just too much for two old people to bear, he wanted to tell her.

"Do you think that she'll hurt him?" He laughed a little, thinking of Henrie taking Trevor to task. "He might not be in love with her right now, but I'm betting that he's about as close as he's ever been before."

"I don't know what to think about the two of them, do you?" She shook her head, asking him if he thought that Trevor was someone that she could love. "I don't know why not. I mean, he's a good man and seems to have his head out of his bottom all the time. He certainly did look like he was worried for her when we got to the hospital. My goodness, wouldn't that just set her up nicely? I'd really like to be around when she has children."

She picked up her spoon to taste her soup.

"I guess we both should be taking better care of ourselves and eating better." He tasted his soup and found that it was delicious. Not only did he eat all the soup, but he'd made a big dent in his salad as well.

It was nice to have all the greens in a bowl mixed up. Their cook usually put them in little piles in the bowl, making it hard for him to taste it all. "I'll have to have this done for me at home. I love having all of it mingled around."

Trevor joined them just as they were splitting a piece of lemon pie. He said that they'd given her something for pain, and she'd be out for a few hours. When he got up to get himself something to eat, Henry thought of all the things that he wanted to ask him, especially in light of how he was acting around Henrie. As soon as he sat down, Henry asked him about her.

"I don't know what I feel about her." Anna asked him if he liked her. "Very much so. I find myself thinking of things that I'd like to do with her just to make her upset with me. I haven't any idea why that is fun for me but I'm learning when to back off too. She has a nice temper on her, doesn't she?"

"Don't hurt her." Anna took his hand when he said that to Trevor. "She's all we have in the world right now. Her momma, she's a good woman, but she doesn't come around all that often. And I don't remember the last time I saw our son. But Henrie, she's been our rock since…well, since she's been born."

"I have no intentions of hurting her, but that's something that I can't promise. Like I said, I don't know how I feel about her, but I do find that I want to be with her. Even when she's yelling at me to go home and get some sleep." He laughed a little, and it made him smile. "I really do find her to be my good luck charm. She told me that Peabody was aiming at me when she stepped in front of him. She might not have saved my life—I don't know if he would have killed me or not. But she certainly didn't allow me to get hurt like she is. I owe her for that, if nothing else."

"I did know that. She told us that she was wrestling the gun from him when she felt a burning pain. I'm not saying that I'm glad it was her, but she more than likely saved a great many people from getting hurt by what she did." He said he'd thought the same thing when she'd told him what had happened. "I know that he's dead, but I can't imagine someone shooting at someone else for the price of a bunch of furniture. What is this world coming to right now? It's just chaos. Henrie said she didn't understand them either."

The three of them talked for a little while. Trevor enjoyed the soup as much as they did, but instead of a salad like they had, he had two burgers with the works. Oh, to be young again, he thought.

The three of them headed back to Henrie's room and he had to admit, he did feel a good deal better after eating. The company was good, too, so he felt like he could handle seeing his little girl again. But he couldn't.

As soon as he saw her with the oxygen on and a monitor watching her heart, he broke down again. She was just too young to be going through this kind of trauma, and he wished that it had been him lying there instead of her.

It was nearly sunrise when they went home. He was glad for Trevor driving them home. He might well have fallen asleep while driving as it was he was dozing at each stoplight and could have caused an accident. That would have been just like him to get hurt when he was needed the most.

"I'll come and get you tomorrow, too, if

she's not released. Would that be all right?" Before he could answer, Anna did. Telling him that she was grateful for him thinking about the two of them. "It's all right. I know that worrying about Henrie would make you distracted. I know it does me a bit."

"Thank you, young man." He shook hands with Trevor and headed into the house. He was so exhausted he thought he could sleep standing up. As he was getting ready for bed, all he could think about was sleep. Even as he laid his head on his pillow, Anna already asleep, he knew that the days were just going to be getting harder on the three...maybe four of them. He was really grateful for the extra help in the way of the Strong family.

~*~

Henrie didn't want to move. But they were telling her that she needed to or she could get complications from the surgery that would have her in the hospital for several more days to weeks. Walking down the hallway, holding onto her IV pole, she was making her second trip around when someone came up beside her. It was, of course, Trevor.

"Are my grandparents here?" He said that he had made sure that they had a limo to come in to see her, but no, they hadn't slept well, so they were taking it easy now that she was up and around. "They said that I could get pneumonia if I don't get up and move around. I'm doing that. Alone if you don't mind."

"I don't mind keeping you company. She tried her best to ignore him but it was difficult when he smelled so good. "They say if you keep progressing like you are that you might get to go home tomorrow or the next day. I'd tell them it's because you're stubborn, but I think they already know that."

"Jade came in to see me. She said that I had to have extra juice to keep me under. I guess it has something to do with me being a redhead. Why aren't you at work or something?" He said that he was self-employed and could come and go as he pleased. "I bet that's not the least bit true. I'm self-employed, too, but I don't just come and go as I please. I'd be broke if I did that. What are you really missing out on?"

"I had three meetings today with investors. One of them said that they had a better deal with the bank. That's fine. I'm betting that the bank won't be as accommodating as we've been before for him. The second meeting I canceled to be here with you. The third one isn't until dinnertime, but I have a feeling that he's going to bail on me as well. After reading about the shooting in the center, people are thinking that I need to regroup. All I can think about is that you saved my life. You did, too." She told him that he shouldn't expect that to happen again. "Christ, I hope not. That was the scariest thing that has ever happened, having you hurt like you are."

"Yeah, that's been a lot of fun." She turned to go back down the hall, and the nurse told her that she needed to rest. "I didn't want to walk around in the first place and now you're telling me that I've had enough. You'll have to make up your mind, please. I'm too sore to be doing something that I don't need to be doing."

"You're fine. It's just that too much isn't going to help you anymore than you not walking at all. I just thought you'd like to have a sit down with your boyfriend." She said he wasn't her anything. "If you say so."

She was helped into her room, the too long walk catching up to her. By the time she was able to get something for the pain, she was too out of it to have any kind of conversation with Trevor. She just wanted to close her eyes and have all this over with forever. As soon as she closed her eyes, she knew that Trevor was going to be there when she woke up again.

Waking up, jerking awake, she cried out in pain. If she'd known that her grandparents were there, she could have stopped it. They were worried enough right now, and she hated adding to their being upset. Grandda tried to help her sit up, but he was only making it worse. Trying her best not to snap at him, she was glad for Trevor stepping in and making it better. Not that she'd tell him that. The little shit even winked at her as if he knew what she was thinking.

"I thought you had a meeting or something." He said that he had to cancel because of one of his pups. "You didn't hurt it, did you? I bet they're loving you not being there all the time. They can tear things up for you."

"No, I had to take him to the vet. I was sitting at the kitchen table when they came in, all playful. When they turned around, seeing their reflection in the oven door, they tried to protect me by head-butting their reflection. He had to have nine stitches in his big empty head for being a good dog." She asked him if he was going to be all right. "Yes. The vet said that he was going to have a hell of a headache for a few days, but he'll be fine. I allowed him to lie down on the couch, and he and his sister are enjoying that little bit of freedom."

"He'll be bumping his head all the time just to be able to lie on the couch with you." He asked her what she'd do to lie on the couch with him. "Stab you in the back for being so stupid to think that I'd want to be there. Again, don't you have something else to do?"

"Henrietta Lilith Banister. Be nice to him. He's making it so that we can get back and forth to see you, and for that alone, you should be nice to him about. What am I going to do with you?" Trevor asked if her name was Henrietta. "Yes. She was named after her father who was Henry too. But it's confusing at times, I must say to have two Henry's and a Henrie in the house."

"I love the shortened form of your name. It suits you." She asked him what that was supposed to mean. "Nothing. You're more of a Henrie than a Henrietta. A beautiful version of your grandfather. I love it."

He was irritating her, and she was sure that he was doing it on purpose. Why he'd want her to be pissed off at him—she wondered then if it was because he wanted her to push him away. Just like a man, irritating someone so that they'd be the injured party rather than the woman. She found herself wanting to be nice to him so that it would backfire on his plans. Whatever they were.

He left just after noon. He needed to check on his dogs. He told her that he'd be back with dinner for them all. Grandda and Grandma said they were going to go home soon, too, as they were exhausted and needed to get a nap.

She was glad that they weren't driving home. It was good of the Strong family to provide them with the limo. She'd never been in one, but Grandda made it sound like it was a luxury that he'd enjoy again if given the opportunity again.

It wasn't as if he couldn't afford one if he wanted. Every Christmas, he would make plans to ride in one to go see the Nutcracker in Columbus, but something always came up, and they'd just drive there like normal. It was fun, really, figuring out what was going to happen the following year to mess up his plans. The last time, it had been because he'd forgotten to make reservations for one. The year before that, he'd not wanted to give the driver his cold, so they drove. And the following week, they were all sick with his cold.

She loved her grandparents so much, but they were silly too.

Jade came in to see her, and she said she was doing great. If she didn't have any troubles tonight, then she saw no reason for her to stay. Then she mentioned Trevor and how he was upset about his dog.

"Yes, poor thing. He told me about him. Will he be all right?" She said pretty much what she'd said and that the dogs would be doing it more often to be pampered a bit. Then she mentioned the house.

"He's moving in this weekend. We're all going to be there helping with his few things. Then he's going to order take away so that we can be the first to eat in his home. You can go if you behave yourself." She asked her why she'd be invited. "I don't know if anyone has told you this or not, but we are all thinking that he's falling in love with you." She stared at her for a full minute.

"I don't know what to say about that. I mean, we're barely friends and haven't really spent all that much time together." She said that it had happened like that for her and Jenson. And that she really didn't care for him all that much when they first met. "It's not that I don't care for him. I like him all right. He likes to piss me off for some odd reason. Why do you think that he's in love with me?"

"He told his brother." She didn't know what to say about that, so she didn't voice her concerns about her being different than he was. Also, she thought that he could do much better than her since she was someone who didn't care for people all that much. "You're thinking too hard. Just let it go and see where it takes the two of you."

"I've been…I was literally left at the altar a few years ago. Basically, we didn't love one another but it was a convenience for the two of us. I'd get my dad off my back, and he'd get the same from his parents. He needed to marry before he was twenty-two, and we were set to marry the day before." She asked if she had loved him. "No. I mean, neither of us loved each other. As I said, it was for convenience more than anything."

"So he hurt you because he left you standing there. You more than likely dodge a bullet with that one." She said she found out later that he'd been in love with his best man, and they ran off together. "I've heard of that happening before. Yeah, you dodge a huge bullet with that man. So, what does that have to do with Trevor? I don't think he's secretly in love with anyone but you."

"You keep saying that. I don't—I don't really understand love. Or the implications of being in love. It seems like a messy deal. Two people get together, get married after a time then they have kids. Being about as miserable as they were before they married." She looked at her. "What makes you think that you're in love with your husband? I mean, do you think about him all the time? Could be that you're just waiting for him to fuck up so that you can run off."

"Could be, but I don't think so. What makes me feel like I'm in love? That's a good question. Yes, I do think about him all the time. It doesn't matter what I'm doing either; a thought will pop into my head about him, and I'll get all tingly. If you tell anyone I said that, then I'll hunt you down. He makes me want to be a better person. You don't know this, but I'm a mean bitch when I want to be." Henrie said that couldn't be true. She was so nice. "Very funny. Yeah, I think you're a great deal like me. Hurt and using meanness to hide your pain. I believe that you're hurting because of something that was done to you—other than your ex. Could it be your parents? No, not your mom. How about your dad, is it someone that is in your life when you don't want him around?"

"He tried to have my mom abort me because he was a Banister, and she wasn't. Turned out that they got married for me to have a Banister last name but I've never really gotten into the money part of my last name. And there is plenty of that." She told her that the Strongs were worth billions. "So am I."

Jade didn't say anything for which she was glad. Henrie had worked hard for herself and invested well. Then there was the trust fund that she had when her father passed away, and her mom had put her in her will so that she would get what she left behind as well. Mom was a better investor than she was.

"So it's not the money that has you thinking that you and him aren't suited." She told her that she never said they weren't suited. She just didn't understand the falling in love part. "I don't know how to help you with that. I mean, you do know that your grandparents are in love. I'm sure you've seen all of us being around our husbands. I don't understand why you don't just allow yourself the freedom to fall in love with Trevor."

"Perhaps I will. I'm in no hurry to fall in love. I like him. Kinda. He's sappy at times like he's a teenager that has seen boobs for the first time in his life." They both laughed, and Henrie was happy that she didn't tell her that she knew that he'd seen lots of boobs. "My grandma had an affair once when she and Grandda were younger. I know that he's forgiven her, but she's never forgiven herself for it. I don't know how I'd feel if Trevor, if we got together, were to have an affair. I'd more than likely wring his neck. That's another thing about love. How could two people profess to be in so much love with the other person and step out? Grandma didn't have an answer when I asked her. She said that she had no idea that things with her friend would go so far. I think it only happened the one time, and there was no sex involved. She just went out with him to be going out with him, she told me."

"I could never do that to Jenson. He's my world." Henrie nodded. "What does that mean? He is my whole world."

"It didn't mean anything. I was just agreeing that you are in love with him." Henrie leaned back in the bed and smiled. "You're not like other women I've had this conversation with. They usually get pissed off and leave. It's a good way to shove people out of your life is to question their love for someone."

"Were you trying to get under my skin?" Henrie said that she didn't start out that way, but she was sorry if she offended her. "You didn't. I was enjoying talking to you about love. But I do think that given the time, or if you allow him into your heart, you'll figure out that Trevor has a lot of love he can give you."

"I thought you were going to tell me he was a good catch." She laughed and stood up. Jade was a nice person, and she hoped they could remain friends even if there was nothing between her and Trevor. "So I can still go home tomorrow?"

"You can. But I'm to understand that you're going to be staying with your grandparents. I'd not do that if I were you. They already say how tired they are just from visiting you. They're going to work themselves into a heart attack if they have you around to fuss over. They're wonderful people but it will hurt them physically for you to be there full time with them." She asked her if she thought that she was going to move in with Trevor. "What an excellent plan. Yes, I'll tell Trevor that you suggested it. I'm sure that he'll be thrilled to have you there."

"I didn't say that. Not at all." Jade kissed

her on the cheek and told her that she'd be better than anyway because of how she was going to be getting around. "I can live anywhere that's not Trevor's new home. Hell, I'd stay in a hotel if that's what you think would work for me. Jade? Jade, come back here and tell me what you're going to tell Trevor. I never said that I'd — damn it, woman. You're too pushy. Get back here."

Jade was more than likely laughing all the way to her car about how she had tricked her. And it was a dirty trick, too. She didn't want to live with him any more than he'd want her living there. It was his new home, and she was positive that he didn't want strange women sticking around because she was hurt and couldn't be left alone.

Chapter 5

He could tell that Henrie didn't want to be sitting on the couch while the rest of them brought things into the house. He'd had the furniture people put the couch on last so it would come off first so that she could have something to sit on while they were unpacking. It worked out well for her. Jade wouldn't even allow her to walk around because she said she'd pick something up to help.

Looking down at the boxes he had in his hands, Trevor thought perhaps he'd gone a little overboard on the essentials he'd gotten, like toilet paper, paper towels, and such. His mom was still laughing when she put them in the pantry. There were so many of them.

"Hello?" He went to the living room to see what Henrie needed, and she asked him for a glass of water. "It's kind of dry in here. Didn't they tell you that you had a whole house humidifier?"

"I turned the downstairs furnace off because of the doors being open all the time. I think that was a mistake. The upper floors have their own furnace, and I left it alone. But it's cold down here, don't you think?" She pointed out that she had the fireplace going, so it wasn't too cold. "I'll have to turn it back on to see if that humidifies the house more. I'm glad you mentioned that. I might have forgotten."

Giving her a glass of water and several bottles so she could have them as well, he was excited about how well the house was coming along. The dining room looked complete because he'd been able to unearth his grannie's dinnerware set to put in the room. His mom and Jade had put that all away for him after they'd run things through the dishwasher. The table that he'd gotten gleamed in the dining room, and he loved that he'd been able to get it.

Jade told him that Henrie could get up and walk around now that the boxes were in the house but said that she couldn't lift even a loaf of bread. It would hurt her in ways that she'd wish she was still in the hospital. So while his kitchen appliances, he'd forgotten how many he'd purchased were being put away, he walked around the main floor with her to keep her out of trouble. He should have figured that she'd be all right with not lifting. She said she was still sore from the surgery.

"I can't believe how much it looks different. I thought it looked really good when the previous owners were still here but you've really changed it up. I love the butcher block you have instead of an island." He told her that it had been his grandmother's when she was alive. "It's perfect." She stopped moving when they were in the pantry, looking around. "You're sure you don't mind me staying here? I don't want to put you out or anything. And I'm in no shape to fend you off, so please don't get frisky with me. I'm a wounded person." He laughed.

"No, I'll not get frisky with you until you say it's all right. I want to, don't get me wrong on that, but I don't want you injured any more than you are now. You need to get better. How will you eat more than your weight in food next week if you're hurting." She looked confused. "It's Thanksgiving. Did you forget?"

"I did, actually. I wonder what my grandparents are going to be doing. I usually eat with them." He told her how his mom had invited them to their home for dinner and football. "Grandda loves football and food. Grandma watches it and pretends to not know anything about the game, but if there is a bad call, she gets all worked up."

Trevor wanted to kiss her but knew that there wasn't a worse time for him to try. While walking around with her, he pointed out some of the things that he'd had done to the pantry and showed her the oversized freezer that his brother Jenson had suggested that they have put in.

"It'll come in handy during the summer months. The cook — I've forgotten her name, said that she would use the gardens in the back for fresh things. She also unearthed a herb garden that she plans on utilizing. I can't wait." He guided her to the back yard where his pups — Pebbles and Bam-bam, were playing after she told him that the cook's name was May. She asked him about his dogs' names. "Oh, that was Gracie. She named them after the cartoon The Flintstones. She said she didn't watch it as a child; it was before her time, but Sherm, her son, was enjoying them. Jenson has Barney and Betty. Clay took a pair that were called Fred and Wilma. The others are named after the cartoon as well, but for Blackie. She had named her first when she saw them and couldn't change her name. She's the bossy one of the group."

"How adorable." The dogs were all over

Henrie when she sat down on one of the chairs that he'd purchased. They weren't careful, but she didn't seem to mind. They were having a good time and she was laughing harder than he'd thought he'd ever heard before.

Getting her back inside, she sat down on the couch and nearly fell asleep in mid-sentence when she was talking to him about the dogs. They were getting bigger daily, and now that they were a few weeks older, he could leave them in the house in their crate for longer periods of time.

Dinner was a lot of all kinds of things. They would order that way so as not to overwhelm one restaurant. There was pizza, of course, as well as Chinese and Mexican food. He had downed three soft tacos before he remembered to go and wake up Henrie. She was still resting and he debated about waking her when she suddenly opened her eyes to look at him.

"Something is wrong." He told her no, he'd just come to get her for dinner. "I'm sorry I keep falling asleep. Jade said that I'm still working through the drugs I got in the hospital. I don't know what it is, but I'd like to be awake for more than ten minutes at a time."

"You were awake for a whole three hours

this time. Good for you." She glared at him, and he had to laugh. He was going to point out that his mom was better at that than she was, but she was too close to him, and his mom was as well. Barton got up when she came into the dining area when it was obvious that he was going to need to get some extra chairs if everyone was going to be eating with them.

There were the helpers that he'd gotten by advertising at the local school that he was going to need help. He was glad that Barkley had suggested that he hired a few high school kids to help out bringing things in and breaking down boxes. They were saving for a car, he'd been told.

He was putting the linens away when his dad found him. After getting one of his famous hugs, he asked him what he thought about the house. Dad said that he was proud of him for finally getting out of the condo. It was no place to raise a family if you didn't have to.

"Do you think she'll want a family?" He asked his dad, who, knowing full well who he was talking about. "Henrie, you goof. Have you even told her that you love her yet?"

"No. Mostly because we're getting used to one another. To be honest, Dad, I'm not sure why my brothers haven't been teasing me. Especially Jenson. Just last week, I told them that I was never going to find someone to love, and the next afternoon, there she was." He laughed a little. "She's great, don't you think? I mean, even if you don't consider that she saved my life, she is wonderful to be around."

"Your mother was just saying the other day that she likes that she fits in so well with the other women. I think she was saying that she's just as sarcastic as the others. But I'd not ask her about that." Trevor told his dad that he didn't have a death wish. "No, you're a good deal smarter than that. What are you going to do about her being wealthy? I mean, from what Jade was able—"

"Don't tell me." He nodded and said he was sorry. "Don't be sorry. I just want to learn about her the old fashion way. Through the two of us getting to know one another. And I do want to get to know her before we get too far along in what I feel for her."

"You love her." Even though it wasn't a question he told his dad that he did love her. Very much. "But she doesn't know if she loves you. That's something else I heard."

"Henrie told me about the conversation that

she had with Jade. I might have been offended if not for how hard she was laughing about it. Jade said it caught her off-guard. It was her that was usually the one that was grilling someone about feelings." Dad laughed again with him. "I think that Jade was a little pissy that she'd been able to do that to her. I love it for no other reason than it's to see that Jade can be had. I believe that they'll be the best of friends now."

"I think they all want to welcome her into the family but are waiting on a signal from you." He said he could see that. "Good. The sooner you get your ducks in a row or whatever it is you're working with, we can have another wedding and have a good time. I bet she'd have her grandda walking her down the aisle and crying the entire way. He's an emotional man and I have respect for him for allowing others to know that about him."

"I really like the two of them as well. Henry told me that he's been emotional since the day she was set in his arms. I can see that, too. The two of them would have been in their fifties, I think, and would have welcomed her with open arms. They're good people, I think." Dad said he enjoyed being around them as well. "Good. One less thing that has to be worried about. Everyone is happy."

It didn't take long for the house to be set to rights. They were short three lamps for the living room, and he forgot to order a grill for them to eat out on the patio this summer. But he did have towels to bathe with, as well as dishwasher detergent, which he thought was a good thing. And he'd also remembered to get a vacuum as well as a dust mop so that he could take care of the hardwood floors in most of the house. Mom asked him about the apartment that is over the garage.

"I was going to ask the Banisters if they wanted to live there. I can have an elevator put in with no problem because it's so open in the back end. It'll be just for them, and I think they'll enjoy being close to us." Mom told him that was a brilliant idea. "Yeah? I have them on occasion."

"Smart ass." She smacked him on the arm and hugged him. His parents had always been huggers, and he knew why. Mom's mother had been standoffish and cold and would only allow them to hug her if she had on a large towel so as not to mess up her outfits. After much more of that, they stopped hugging her altogether. It was just too much work to get a hug that seemed to not mean all that much to her. "I'm going to have some company over in a few days. We're working on the baskets for the holidays. Do you think that Henrie will be well enough to help us out?"

"I don't know. You'd have to clear it with Jade. She's been keeping a close eye on her and her moving around. I don't think I've ever broken a rib, but I can't imagine that it's all that easy to get over." Mom told him that she'd had a broken rib before, and it took her months to get to where she wasn't hurting every time she had to move. "Then I think you have your answer. But I'd invite her over. If you don't mind. That way, she can be a part of the family without having to injure herself by hanging out."

"Good idea." Mom kissed him again before leaving him to sort out the things in the pantry, and that was when Henrie joined him.

Once she closed the door, he felt his heart race a bit. It was the first time that they'd been alone anywhere in the house, and he was slightly nervous. He asked her if she was all right. Shaking her head and then nodding, he smiled at her.

"If you were to ask me that question right now, I'd have the same answer. Really. How are you feeling? Are you in pain?" She said that she was, but it was tolerable. "Good. Don't overdo it too much. You're on the mend now and—"

"Will you kiss me? I know that people are saying that you're in love with me, and I'm coming to the conclusion that I don't mind that so much." He cocked a brow at her. "Give me a minute. This is all just coming to me. I've been kissed before. I mean, plenty of times if you count my parents and grandparents. But I have a feeling that it's going to be really different with you. Like...I don't know, just different."

"I would love to kiss you." He took a step toward her, putting the boxes of cereal he had in his hands on the shelf. "Are you talking about a kiss like your parents give you?" He kissed her on the forehead, then her cheek. "Or your grandparents might give you?" He kissed her firmly on her cheek and then looked at her. They were only a few inches apart by then. "I don't want you to be disappointed in me if I give you the wrong kiss."

"I doubt that anyone has been disappointed in your kisses." She put her hand on his shoulder. "Remember to be careful of my ribs and kiss me like you mean it."

He kept telling himself as he was lowering his head toward hers that he couldn't take advantage of her right now. He knew that he could hurt her, and he didn't want their first of what he hoped were many kisses ruined because he had pulled her too close to him.

As soon as his lips touched hers, he felt her tongue slide across his lips. Gentling his movements to match hers, he was glad now that she had shut the door. Christ, he was in love with this woman.

He didn't pull away, but he didn't press her to him either. Careful of his every move, Trevor decided that if he didn't end this soon, he'd have her pressed against the nearest wall and have her naked before too much longer. Instead of taking the chance, he held her while she laid her head on his chest. Even that seemed to be pushing him into wanting more from her.

"I was wrong about your kisses." He started to ask her what he'd done wrong, but she spoke before he could. "You're much better than I've ever known, and I'm reasonably sure that you've been devastating women all your life with your mouth."

It caught him so off guard that he threw back his head and laughed. Kissing her again, quickly on her mouth, he held onto her while he put the cereal onto the proper shelf and opened the door to leave. His mom and grandma were in the kitchen and he kissed them both on the cheek as well. It was cause for celebration.

He was the best kisser known to men and women. Laughing again, he was happier than he'd ever been. Finding his future wife was like having his cake and all the icing in the store, too. Yes, he thought to himself. He was deliriously happy.

~*~

Sitting in the office, Henry was as nervous as he'd ever been. Today, they'd started on the elevator that would get him and his lovely wife up to their apartment, and he was excited about that, too. His emotions were all over the place today, and he didn't know how to calm himself down. Sitting on his hands usually worked but today nothing was. The doctor had called him in, especially today and he didn't care for that.

Once a month, Henry had to go and get bloodwork done. He'd been a diabetic for the last ten years, and because of Anna, his A1C, glycated hemoglobin, or the measurement of his blood sugar levels. His numbers had been right on the dot for it not getting worse since they'd begun testing him. But today, just this morning, he'd been called and asked to come in. The call had taken him from work, too, something that he never did before.

"Dr. Weston will see you now." Nodding at the pretty little receptionist, he made his way into the office. He wished now that he'd asked Anna to come with him, but he'd not told anyone where he was going, just in case. In case, what? He hadn't any idea but he knew now that was the dumbest thing— "Mr. Banister?"

"I'd like to call someone in to be with me. It might be nothing at all, but I want to call someone. Do you think you could be put off for a few minutes while I call someone?" She smiled and told him that would be fine. "Thank you. I'll let you know if it doesn't work out."

"You go ahead and call who you wish, Mr. Banister. I'll just take a patient back early. Mr. Todd is always early, hoping to get out earlier. I think he does this to win something from his wife. You go ahead and make your call, and I'll bring you in as soon as he or she gets here." He went to sit down and make his call while she called in Mr. Todd.

"Hello? Henry? Is something wrong?" He nearly wept when he heard Trevor on the other end. After telling him what was going on, he laughed a little. "I'm in town now, as a matter of fact. I can be there in just a couple of minutes, ten at the most."

"Thank you, son. Thank you so much. Don't tell the women. I just want to get the news and deal with it on my own for a few minutes before I have to talk to them. They'll pester me to death with questions, and I know that I won't have the answers. Maybe you can listen, and you'll be able to help me out."

"You're thinking that this isn't going to be him telling you that your diabetes is gone, am I right?" He said that he'd been feeling off for a bit and thought that he was going to tell him something more. "I'll be there for you. And I can understand wanting someone there to remember for you. My dad does that and sometimes goes with people to the doctor to hear the news. I'll be there soon."

The relief that he felt had him feeling a little guilty. Asking him to what he thought of was a lie to his wife and granddaughter. However, this was important. He didn't know why, but he was worried that he had cancer. It had been something that had taken his older and younger brothers when they'd been young men and his mother. He didn't want to know, but he knew that it was important too. As soon as Trevor opened the office door, he held onto him like he was a lifeline. And he was for him in that moment. A lifeline to a better life, he hoped.

True to her word, the receptionist took him back as soon as Trevor arrived. They were sitting in the little room when one of the nurses came in and took his vitals. His blood pressure was a little high, and he told her that he was nervous. She never gave him a reason not to be. Just telling him to relax, and she'd take it again.

"I don't know that you'll find the numbers to be all that different. I'm still nervous." She said that it was the same, and he was going to have to keep from getting himself worked up. Like that was going to happen when your doctor clears a time for you to come in the same day. Usually, it was weeks before a person could get in to see him. Bidding his time, he was glad that there wasn't a clock in the room, or he might have been—

"Henry." He looked at Trevor when he stood up. "Henry, you don't know what he's going to say to you and you're worked up enough to give yourself a heart attack. Breathe in and out and try to think of something else. Like what you're going to be doing when the great-grandchildren come along."

"You two having a baby right away?" He asked him if he knew what Henrie wanted to do.

"I don't know, really. I know that she wanted kids at one time, but I don't know—you have no idea how much I'd love to see one of my great-grandchildren being born. Oh my the fun I'll have with them. I'll get to tell them all about their mommy. And about you too. I'd love another little girl like Henrie was but a little boy that looks like you? Well, that would make me prouder than a speckled pup under a little red wagon, it would."

"Right now, we're just waiting on her ribs to get better. I'd marry her today if I thought that she'd say yes." He said that he could tell that she was falling in love with him. "Really? Oh, I can't wait to tell her that I love her. I'm giving her time, you see. I don't want to rush her into anything just yet."

They talked for another twenty minutes, and he felt better. His head was beginning to pound, and his chest was hurting a little bit. Glad now more than ever that he'd brought Trevor into his circle, Henry decided that whenever he had to get bad news, if this was bad news or had to make a decision, he was going to have him at his side. Trevor was calming and smart. The man would treat his baby girl the best when they got married and into love.

The nurse came in and took his blood pressure again, and it was within margin. It made him feel so much better that before she left the room, she took it again for him. It was what it usually was, a nice low pressure, and even that took some of the edge off his fear. He looked at Trevor when she left the two of them alone again.

"Hello, Henry. How are you feeling?" And just like that, the doctor coming in, he felt like he was going to have a heart attack again. Doctor Weston tsked at him and told him that this wasn't the end of the world. "You'll see we've come so far in medical procedures since your family was diagnosed."

"I have cancer." Doctor Weston said that he didn't know that yet, but his blood numbers were a concern. "What do you have to do to find out what is wrong? I'll do it. You know I will. Henrie is going to be marrying soon and I've made plans to be around when the children come."

"And you will be if you stop worrying over little things. I just said your blood numbers were concerning. That doesn't mean you have cancer. It might just be you have an infection or something. Let's not burn down bridges until we have all the tests back." He told him that he didn't know if he could do that. "Well, then, I think it's a good thing that you have Trevor Strong with you here. He comes from a good family, and his father is a good man. The entire family are people that you can depend on. I just want you to go over to the hospital today and have some more extensive tests done. Also, an MRI as well as a CAT scan."

Arrangements were made, and he was going to go straight over to the hospital and be admitted. Only because the stress test would need to be done first thing in the morning, and they wanted him rested — by medication so that he'd tolerate the test better. It was time to call his wife and Henrie and he didn't even want to do that. Trevor said that he didn't mind and that he could call them both at the same time and it would be better. They could ask him questions, and he'd be able to answer them both at the same time. Henry loved that idea and fell a little deeper in love with the young man more than he had before. He really was a good man.

They were both surprisingly calm when Trevor talked to them. He thought it was because he wasn't emotional like he would have been. Telling them what the doctor said, even about medical treatments coming a long way, he had them calmly coming in with the family limo. That way, they didn't have to worry about them driving and getting into an accident.

As soon as they all hung up, Trevor told him he was ready and that he'd be already in his room when they arrived. Good. He thought that would be easier on him, too. Not having to push anyone out of his room when he was getting his gown on. Then he remembered that his wife was bringing him some pajamas, and he'd feel better with his own pillow, too. Trevor had thought of everything.

He was in a gown, what they preferred him to be in when his wife and granddaughter arrived. Not only had she brought him his clothing, but he had his kit too, shaver, deodorant and other necessities. Since he didn't need to be in the bed just yet, he pulled on his pants so that he'd not forget himself. They had more questions when Anna and Henrie arrived and Trevor got a nurse to come in and answer them for them all four. He was going to adopt Trevor, he told his wife. Of course that helped as well, breaking the tension that had been in the room.

Just when his wife was making up her bed in one of the chairs, he was taken down to get the scans done. While he'd never had an MRI before, he was glad that the nurse had warned him that it was going to be loud. After that test, he did feel a little nervous again, and the nurses' station, as he passed by there, told him that they had a little bit of something to help him relax. As soon as they put it into his IV, he could feel it working. It was just the ticket. He was feeling much better about all the crap going on.

Since Anna was going to spend the night in the room with him, he did try to get her to go home, he was ready for a little television and then bed. Getting into the bed with him, she and he watched their favorite newscasters as well as a couple of game shows. After the news, however, Trevor and Henrie left, telling him that they'd be there in the morning first thing. His first test was scheduled for eight, and that was fine with him.

Twice in the middle of the night, they woke him up to take his blood pressure and other vitals. Anna didn't wake either time, for which he was grateful, and was glad that one of them was getting a good night's sleep. Whatever happened tomorrow, one of them had to be on their toes. As soon as he was going back to sleep, he came to a decision that he thought Anna could take care of for him. He was going to put Trevor in charge of the money that he was leaving to charities and that would give his heart a little better feeling. He trusted his attorney, but he wanted something that had a vested interest in his life to make sure that the charities got what he wanted them to. And he knew that Trevor would be that man.

By the time the sun came up the next morning, he was ready for his day of tests. Doctor Weston was coming in to see him at noon to go over things, and he was glad about that, too. So far, things hadn't been too bad, but Henry was glad that his little family was right there with him. As soon as he got back from his stress test, feeling slightly run down, he was also glad to see that Trevor's parents had come in and brought food for them.

Henry had really fallen into a good family with this one and he thought perhaps he was the luckiest man in the world right now. He also knew that whatever came of the tests, he was glad that he had all the support that he did with the Strong family and his wife and granddaughter. Yes, sir, he thought, he was a lucky man.

Chapter 6

Trevor thought that he'd sleep for a month. Henry had been in the hospital for a week now, and they were finally ready to free him. The man had had a great deal done to him and all he wanted to do was to go home and rest in his own bed.

The elevator had been finished up just the day before. Not only was the apartment set up for the two of them but Trevor had turned the bottom part of the garage into a large open area so that the two of them could entertain while they lived there. After all the weatherizing had been put in and carpets put onto the lower floors, he'd had a gas fireplace put in so that they could have company over as well. With a kitchen on the top floor and bottom, the two of them could do just what they wanted and live out their lives without a bit of problem. Even after the surgery had been performed, they were both excited to be going home to their new place.

"I'm so glad that the two of them will be

close. After that scare, I want them close so that I can see them both daily, if not more." Trevor told her that he liked seeing them daily as well. "It was brilliant of your parents to get them that golf cart. Now they don't have to walk from their home to ours. I have to do something really nice for them."

It turned out that Henry did have two tiny spots on his liver. After setting up the surgery so that they could look at them to rule out cancer, they found one on his right kidney as well. The surgery was long, three hours, because they were doing a full search while they had him open and taking care of the spots. After removing them, all five, they ended up finding were sent off to be analyzed. They'd know the results in a couple of days, but Weston was saying that he thought they were cysts and not cancer at all.

Trevor thought that all of them were worn out. He knew that he was. Between the hospital and work, he thought that he was sleeping standing up most of the time. But his job was something that he went to when things got scary at the hospital, and he wished that Anna had something like that. As it was, Henrie was running the shipping company and going to the hospital for her grandma three times a day. It was wearing on everyone.

"I know that we've been sharing a house. I would also like to share a bed with you." He nodded, not sure where this was going, when Henrie turned to him when they were in the elevator going up to Henry's floor to take him home. "I don't mean sex right now. I'm still incredibly sore, but I think that once I'm rested up, and you are too, I'll be a good deal better. I've been stressing and hurting since this all began — don't tell my grandparents — that I think that's what is keeping me from getting better. I've enjoyed running the business, but I can't do both of them like this all the time. I need something to go better."

"I agree. I've been working, too, and every time I go there, I find myself napping at my desk for a few minutes. The computer is usually asleep when I wake but I keep telling myself that it's because it just turned off. For all I know, I could be napping for an hour." They both laughed, and he kissed her on her mouth. "I would love to sleep with you. And I'm just too tired enough that there will be no getting frisky, at least on the first few nights. I want a nice big bed and you to warm me up."

Thanksgiving was tomorrow, and he was happy that his mom had told him not to make anything like the others were doing. Just getting back and forth and through the day was taking up most of his time. Cooking a side dish sounded like it was too much. But when he'd been home this afternoon after work, May, their cook, said that she'd talked to his mom, and she was going to make some macaroni and cheese for him to take over. It was the best news he'd heard all day besides getting to sleep with his favorite roommate.

That's why he was glad that he was going to be going home after getting Henry and Anna set up. They'd hired a cook for them as well so that they didn't have to work around that chore. Henry was nearly asleep before he was put in his bed, and Anna was out. He noticed that she was a heavy sleeper, and nothing could wake her up if they needed her. But the little bitty sound of the alarm on her phone could bring her right up out of the bed like she'd been tossed from it. It was the funniest thing for him to know.

"I'm exhausted. I don't know that I can eat anything." Trevor told Henrie that she'd better eat something, even if it was just a yogurt, or her body would wake her up before she was rested, and that wouldn't do her the least amount of good.

So, the two of them ate a small sandwich

and finished it off with a vanilla yogurt. Dragging themselves up the stairs to the master suite, he was happy that his house was finished and that they didn't have to make their beds in order to get into it.

All he did was pull off his pants. They were dusty anyway and he didn't want to get the bed dusty too. His tee shirt was on the floor near his pants. Toeing off his socks and shoes, he was crawling into the bed even as Henrie was coming out of the bathroom. Laying his head down on the fluffy pillow, he was closing his eyes even as his body began to shut down. Exhaustion reached up and slapped him unconscious.

He woke up once and was startled because he didn't know where he was. As soon as Henrie rolled into his body, he closed his eyes and was out again. He'd had a thought to get up and go to the bathroom, but once he closed his eyes, he didn't think it was worth getting all worked up about and went to sleep.

Trevor was alone in the bed when he woke up the next time. Henrie's side of the bed was cold, so he knew she'd been up for a while. Also, he didn't see the light on in the bathroom and got himself up and moving. Stretching, something that he loved to do when he got up, Trevor felt better than he had in a while. It wasn't just the sleep, but the bed had helped as well. A new mattress could make all the difference when you were tired.

After taking a long hot shower, he dressed and went downstairs. The house was quiet, and while that didn't bother him, it did make him wonder how much longer he'd been asleep than Henrie. As he was leaving the kitchen, looking for someone, he found an envelope with his name on it in the dining room.

"Hello, love." He liked the sound of that and sat down to read the rest of the note. "Grandda wanted to get up and around today, so I went over to help him. I hope that now that he's home, he doesn't overdo it. I'm just there for moral support, not lifting him out of the bed." She drew him several little hearts before she continued. "I love you, Trevor. I wanted to say that first. If I had gotten up and you weren't home, I'd be nuts trying to find you. But I do love you. I'll be home as soon as I can, or you can come over to the house and help grandda around. I think he just needs to feel like himself again." Then she wrote, "Love you, H."

Making his way to their home, he was excited

about the snow that was coming down. Glad that he didn't need to drive anywhere, he was happy to be able to walk to his parents' home for dinner. As soon as he knocked on the door, he was happy that Henrie answered it. Kissing her on the mouth, then a second time just to make sure that she was happy, he went into the room and looked at the mess that had been strewn all around the living room since yesterday. It was everything that Henry had brought home, flowers and cards, a breathing machine to help him recover. There were blankets, too, that had been brought to Henry from home that needed to be washed up before being put away again. He picked up one of the larger boxes of plants and began distributing them all around the room. Just doing that took care of some of the things just lying about.

"Just leave those, Trevor. I'll get to them later." He told her that the flowers and such needed to be out of the boxes so they'd not die. "I never thought of that. To be honest, I can't believe that so many people sent flowers and planters to the hospital for him. My goodness, I don't know what I'm going to do with them all."

"You could call my mom. She usually organizes things like this to take to shut-ins that don't get pretty things like this. And planters can be broken down by her ladies' committee and made into much easier things to care for." She asked if he knew if she was busy. "Yes, today. It's Thanksgiving."

"Oh my, I completely forgot. Oh, I'm so sorry, Trevor. I don't know that we're going to make it." Henry came out of the bedroom then and asked what they weren't going to make. "Thanksgiving at the Strong house. I completely forgot about it. We'll have to cancel."

"We will not cancel, Anna. I'm not going to die anytime soon, and since I thought I was, I've decided that I'm going to be grabbing life with both hands and doing anything I can to become a vital part of the world. Even if it's stuffing my gullet with food this time of year." Henry looked at him. "You think your parents will be upset if we show up a little less formal? I might be too tired to get into my—never mind. I'm going to dress to the nines. Yes, sir. I'm grabbing all I can from the world and family while I'm still around to do it. Come on, Anna, let's get ourselves all dolled up and have some fun. Trevor, you'll help me, won't you? Might need some help tucking me into my suit if it still fits."

Henry lost some much-needed weight while in the hospital. The man was tall, so he could handle a few extra pounds, but today, he looked to him like an old man who had been through hell and back. Yes, he'd help him, and he was happy to hear that he was going to live his life with gusto, too.

They were a little early to his parents' home. Mom nor Dad seemed to mind as he took the dish that he'd brought over to the kitchen. Setting it down on the counter to be cooked when it was time, he snagged himself some veggies off the platter that had a dip as well and went into the living room where his family was meeting. After hugging both his parents, he sat down next to Henrie. She was talking to her mom.

"You don't have to do that. In fact, I'd rather you didn't think of renting the place we wanted to give to you at all. I wanted you both close, and this is the best way for all of us." Anna said that they might need it for a rainy day. "Grandma, I have enough money for several years of rainy days without you paying rent. Just enjoy being there so that when we have babies, I'll know that I have you to depend on. Why don't you think of it as free babysitting money for me? This way, I can know and depend on the two of you when I need a break."

"Well, I'm going to put the money aside and give it to your children when they come along. I don't suppose the two of you have popped any questions of late? I mean, it's nearly the new year, and it would be nice to have something to plan for the summer months." She said she thought they might get married at the courthouse. "No. Now, you'll have a large wedding to celebrate life. I want you to send out hundreds of invitations, plan the food, and pick out a cake. And just so you remember, I have your mom's wedding dress — no, that won't do. You need your own style and dress. Yes, that'll be the ticket."

"How about we get married now in the courthouse and plan a large reception for when the warmer weather comes around." Anna didn't look like she was going to agree with that either, so he smiled at her. "If you make me wait until summer to sleep with your granddaughter, we're going to be carrying our child in our arms when we go down the aisle."

"Trevor Martin Strong." His mom laughed when she said that. "You can be so crude when you want to be, I believe. But I can see your point.

It would be difficult for you to wait that long since the two of you are already sharing a house."

"He's not getting frisky with me yet because of all the things that have been going on." She looked at her grandda. "Do you think you can stay healthy for a few months and walk me down the aisle? I'm counting on the two of you. Grandma? You'll have to be my matron of honor when we do this thing. If we do this thing."

"What do you mean if?" Henrie told her that she just wanted to start her life with Trevor and have children that they could watch grow up. "And you won't get married if you have to wait until summer? My goodness, child, you'd do that without the benefit of marriage?"

"Grandma, you're living in the past. People don't have to—I want to be his wife, but I can't wait that long. I want to have children as soon as possible. I want to be large with child and feel it moving within me. Grandma, I want to be everything that you were to me when I came into this world. Grandda being ill scared me into thinking that there isn't as much time as one hopes they can have. We're all going to die, and I want people to say that I was a hell of a person and not who the hell was Henrie Strong anyway? Do you understand?" She nodded and wiped at the tears. "Don't cry, Grandma. I want this to be the best life that I can have, and I want it to start as soon as possible."

"I understand, and I should have thought about not having all that much time left to live. It scared me too, thinking that I was going to lose your grandda. Scared me...I was thinking the same thing, that if I could have some more time, I'd make it so that I left this world a better place than when I came into it. Yes, I understand." Anna hugged Henrie then she hugged him. "You'll be a good husband to her, won't you, Trevor? Take care of our darling little girl for us?"

"I will make it my life's work to make her happier every hour of every day. I'll shower her with love and make sure she knows that I will love her more every day that we have together." He got down on one knee after sliding to the floor and took Henrie's hand into his. "I love you so much, Henrie. And I will forever and beyond. Will you be my wife so that we can start out life together now on this day?"

"Yes. Will you please be my husband, too? And let me pamper you in any way that you'll let me and have lots of children with me? I love you so much, Trevor." She kissed him when he slid the ring on her finger. "Oh, how beautiful. Where did you get this? It looks old."

"It was my grandmother's on my mom's side. Mom got it all being an only child and she let each of us pick out what we wanted of the jewelry. She wasn't a nice person and didn't like us kids all that much, but we tolerated her over the years and that was about all I can tell you about her. Just a bitter old woman." He pulled her up from the floor and held her to him. He winked at her. "We can arrange a marriage as soon as the day after tomorrow. If that's all right with you."

"Yes, perfect." She kissed him this time, right on his mouth. "I love you so much, and I can't wait to have your children and live out what I hope to be a long life with you."

~*~

Dinner was better than she ever could have imagined. There were plenty of leftovers for sandwiches later, and she was enjoying the football games on the largest television she'd ever seen in their living room.

Henrie had to laugh when she saw that her grandda had fallen asleep with a piece of pie in his hands. Grandma was watching the game and eating some of the vegetables that had been on a large platter. Henrie thought for sure that she wasn't going to be able to eat for a week or so.

At around six-thirty, the doorbell rang. Instead of getting up to see who it was, Trevor's parents let him open the door. He didn't know the man, it seemed, but Jade and Jenson did. He was the sitting judge in their town. He was there to marry them.

"So I called in a favor, and he agreed to come here to do it." Trevor was still laughing when he asked his brothers to stand up with him. His dad was his man of honor, and his mom sat with the other women in the living room.

It was nearly over as soon as it started, the judge took home an apple pie that hadn't been cut into yet. After kissing Jade on the cheek, he was gone. It was the most surreal thing that had ever happened to her. I suppose she should be happy that it was halftime of the game, or there might not have been much in the way of witnesses.

Fifteen minutes later, Grandda said that he was ready to go home, and her grandma hugged her tightly before they both left. All the carbs were making them both tired and Grandda needed to check his sugar levels. Trevor was taking them back to their home, and she was glad to be able to help with the cleanup that was made in the kitchen.

"Don't you want to go home too?" She looked at Lisa, confused. Then, when it hit her, she felt her face heat up. "You're a good girl, honey but if you're going to be having babies, you need to go home and start on that."

Never in her life had she been so embarrassed. Of course, she needed to get started on the babies but to have it pointed out to her by her mother-in-law was a bit more than she wanted today. When Trevor called her to tell her that her grandparents were home and safe, she told him not to get out of the car and that they were going home as well. Then she told him that his mom told her that they needed to start on the babies.

"You nearly made me drive off the road." She told him to be careful that she needed him and he laughed. "All right. I'll toot the horn and you come running out. That should give my family something to tease us about for weeks, if not years to come. I love you, babe. I'll be waiting for you to come out of the house in about five minutes."

Watching him pull into the driveway, she kissed Lisa and told her that she'd see her in a couple of days. That was funny to the other woman, and she told her to have fun. Henrie told her that she was planning on having a great deal of fun but not to call unless it was an emergency.

Getting into the car with Trevor, she pulled him to her with a long, and she hoped a very telling kiss. As soon as they parted, she sat on her side of the car and tried not to fidget. All she could think about was getting naked with him and making him know how much she loved him. Trevor was her world, and she wanted him to know that beyond anything else.

It seemed to take forever to get home. The roads were slick, the snow that they'd gotten today was heavy, and she was scared every time they spun out. Even the couple of times that they would slide on the streets, she was terrified that she was going to have to end up in the hospital because they had crashed. When they finally pulled in, she was drenched in sweat, and her nerves were shot.

Putting her head between her legs, Trevor rubbed her back. She could tell that he was nervous as well, but he was handling it better than she was. As soon as she felt like she could get out of the car, they walked hand in hand to the front door, and finally, she felt safe.

She thought that she'd be better off driving

her rig in this weather than in a car. At least with her rig, she did have a bit more weight in the thing and she was driving. Not that Trevor wasn't a good driver, but she needed control over the situation and that would have made her feel so much better.

The house was nice and warm. She realized that she'd forgotten the leftovers that were their share and decided that someone would take them home over going back. In the fridge, there were things that they could make a meal with, but neither of them were hungry.

Trevor went to the living room and turned on the game. She was so disappointed that she wanted to find something heavy and hit him in the head with it. Instead, she went into the living room and sat on the opposite couch. He grinned at her when she huffed.

"I need to unwind after that drive. I would be able to make love to you, but I feel like it wouldn't be the best I want you to have. I'm not sure how you feel, but that's it for me. I might not have mentioned this before, but I hate driving in the snow. It stressed me out enough that I'd need a drink after it. I really hate driving in terrible weather." She asked him if he was going to get a bigger car, one with four-wheel drive. "I never thought of it before, to be honest. If I had to be somewhere, I would just walk. But I doubt very much you'd get very far in those pretty heels. So driving is what we needed. How about tomorrow, we go and get us both a new car, one that I'd feel safe driving in this Ohio weather in with you beside me?"

"That sounds like a plan, but not too early tomorrow. I have plans." He nodded and winked at her again. "Did you know that your winks make me wet?"

Getting up and leaving him there, she made her way to the kitchen again. Fixing them both some sandwiches that she had plans to put in their room for later made her feel pretty good. He seemed to have the upper hand in most things going on between them, and this time she'd done it. Laughing at the expression on his face when he came into the kitchen with her, she asked him if he was all right.

"No. Yes. Did you mean that?" She nodded, pulling out the box of individual chips to take up, too. "You're driving me crazy, you know that, don't you?"

"Of course, it's what I live for. Teasing you after you've been doing the same to me it feels pretty good." He chased her around the table in the kitchen and into the dining room. As soon as he caught up with her, she giggled like a kid. It was a great deal of fun having a husband — Christ, she thought, she had a husband. He asked her what was wrong when she stared up at him.

"We're married." He nodded and asked her if that was all right. "Yes. I've never had a husband before. I just realized that we're married. Isn't that strange?"

"Strange? I guess so if you think about the fact that we've only known one another for about a month. I still love you. Perhaps more now that you're my wife." He smiled at her. "I have a wife. I've never said those words before. It's kind of nice, don't you think?"

"Yes. I can't think of a better person to be married to than you. I only hope that if you get sick of me, you let me know." Trevor said that he could never be tired of her. She was his world. "You say that now. When it's all still fresh."

"I'll be saying it when I'm as old as your grandparents and meaning it even more so. I love you, Henrie Strong, with all my being. My heart only belongs to you. Well, my family, too, but you have the biggest part of it. And when we ever have children, and we can have as many as you wish, I will be bursting with love and happiness because you said yes to me." Holding her in his arms, Henrie felt like she had won the lottery and had everything she'd ever wanted at the same time. "Are you ready to hit the hay? You know, just being around you makes me feel like I could live forever if every day you're there with me."

They walked up the staircase holding hands. They stopped every few steps and touched one another and kissed. Before they were even to the bedroom, her blouse was off, and his shoes were on the steps. Once she kicked her heels off, she felt like she could use a massage.

Standing outside the room, their room, Henrie decided that it didn't matter to her what others thought of their unconventional marriage, the two of them owning a house before they'd been married.

It was just the fact that the two of them were together right now that made her heart skip a few beats. She never knew that love could be so consuming and not enough at the same time. She really did love this man and she knew that he would be hers for as long as he wished. Then he picked her up in his arms and carried her into the room. Again, it was their room and the one that they would share forever.

"I want to undress you." She nodded at him, her breath caught in her throat. "Then, when you're naked, I want to touch every part of you, tasting you as I go. Are you all right with that?"

Her answer was breathless and she was glad that the bed was close so that she could hold onto the posters on it. It was a beautiful bed. The mattress on it was large enough to hold them both without them having to be crowded. Right now, she wanted to be crowded everywhere with him. She wanted to touch him as well, but today, she was going to allow him to take charge and make love to her. She did so love Trevor and hoped that she could show him in the way that she loved him right back.

Chapter 7

"I love you. So much." Before she could tell him how much she loved him again, Trevor was kissing her, making her naked body feel warm from the inside out. Giving her more of his love with each swipe of his tongue, the touch of his fingers over her overheated naked body had her screaming in her head, wondering what was going to happen to her next.

Her breasts ached and felt fuller. When Trevor put his mouth over her nipple, she could only cry out with it. Not in pain, not really, but with undeniable pleasure. As soon as he suckled at her breast, taking it into his mouth, Henrie came screaming out his name. A wonderful heady feeling of love blanketed her in his warmth. She knew that there was more to come, and she couldn't wait for him to give it to her.

"Again, love. Come again for me." She did. So many times that she lost count. Her body, seemingly too exhausted to go on, would rear up and give him what he wanted each and every time he asked. As he moved down her body, his hands making short work of exploring her, she felt her pussy soak the covers beneath her. "I'm going to stretch you for my cock. You told me once that you'd never had sex, so I don't want to hurt you the first time we make love."

Even the word sounded sexy to her. Cock. Something that she desired only from this man in what seemed her entire life. The very fact that he was making this as pleasurable as he could for her, she held her breath when she felt him blowing his warm breath over her entrance.

Trevor took his time making her wetter and wetter until he took her clit into his mouth and nibbled. It was a sensation that denied words to describe it. Even if she could think of any of them, she knew that it would forever be his love that had her rising up from the bed to have him take her once again.

"Mother fuck, yes, oh yes, that's it, Trevor." She roared out her release. It came from her feet through her head and down and out her throat. She was going to be hoarse tomorrow, and she knew that she'd wear it like a badge. He'd done this to her, and she couldn't have been more happy. If she came like this again, she was going to die right here. Telling him that, he only laughed. Then he touched her with his finger, sliding himself in and out of her like she wanted him to do with his cock.

It felt strange at first. An invasion of her girly parts — she had no idea what to call them that sounded as sexy as cock. Then, as he slid quicker in and out of her, she couldn't understand why she'd never had sex before. This was wonderful. Amazing. Awesome. There wasn't anything better than this, she thought. It was then that he took her clit into his mouth again and suckled hard.

She was on a boat that had capsized. Her body was no longer her own. Every part of her, every cell and drop of blood, screamed out for Trevor to stop but to go on as well. As soon as she came a third, then a fourth time, she knew that she was going to die right here and now. Henrie knew too that she didn't care, so long as she died as happy as she was right now. There would be nothing to keep her from it, either.

As he moved up her body, she begged him to stop. Telling him that she couldn't take anything more. But he only had to sit back on his knees, fisting his cock for her that she knew that whatever he did to her next was going to blow her mind. It would be epic enough that she'd beg him every day, every second of every day, for more.

"Don't tense up, love." She did what he asked, spread her legs for him when he moved over her. She was still tense; she could feel it, but he was gentle with her. Telling her how much he loved her, how her cream tasted to him. When he moved his cock at her entrance again, she cried out when he pushed forward. Broke through the barrier that made her no longer a virgin but his other half for life.

Neither of them moved while she tried to deal with the pain. It wasn't as horrific as she'd thought it would be, but it was still painful. Moving her hips to try and get herself in a better position, she moaned when she realized that he had moved with her. It was as if they were connected on some level that only their bodies knew.

"If you keep moving like that, I'm not going to be able to be a gentleman about this and let you get used to me." She looked up at him. His face was granite-hard. The strain of him really being a gentleman was taking a huge toll on him. Moving her hips again, watching his face, she rolled her hips upward and watched the stiffness of his face disappear in a kiss that he gave her.

It didn't take her long to come several times after that. Trevor seemed bent on making her enjoy this more than he was. When he pulled her hips up to meet his on his downward stroke, she held onto his shoulders as if she knew she was going to break apart. When she did, when she came with him, Henrie knew that nothing would ever be the same between them. That they were forever more a couple and that nothing could tear them apart. It hit her hard that what he'd said to her was true. They were one, in love and loving more by the day. Then, she simply blacked out.

Waking in the bed, she was alone. But sitting up, nearly making her sick with the dizziness, she laid back down when he came out of the bathroom. As soon as he snuggled his cool body next to hers, Henrie wrapped her body around his and closed her eyes. The tension that she'd been holding onto for the last several days about sleeping with Trevor was gone. And in its place was pure bliss. Knowing that she was safe, she let sleep take her under. She felt the smile on her face grow when she realized what she'd just done with her husband.

When she woke again, she was alone in the big bed. She could hear Trevor talking in the bathroom and got up to see what he was doing. As soon as he saw her, he smiled hugely and pointed to the bathtub.

The tub was about half full of water and bright green bubbles. She'd picked up the bath bomb a few days ago and hadn't used it as yet. Dipping her toe into the water, she couldn't believe how warm it felt.

As soon as she sat down, her body screamed out in tight muscles and bits of pain here and there. Nothing she thought she couldn't handle. Especially when Trevor sat on the commode next to her. He was smiling at her then he winked.

"How are you feeling? I'm sorry I was so rough on you. Your skin is very easily bruised, isn't it?" She noticed it then. The small finger marks that he'd made on her body. The marks of his teeth on her breast. Henrie touched each of them, remembering what he'd done to her to have marked her in such a way, and it made her shiver.

"I'm going to think of them as badges of honor." She leaned back in the tub and smiled up at him. "Are you going to join me, or am I going to be soaking here all alone."

"If I get into the tub with you, I'm going to take you again. As it is right now, I am holding on dearly to my poor out of shape body until I can rest up." She laughed, asking him what had happened. "First of all, Maverick didn't know that we'd told everyone else not to call us. However, it is nearly three o'clock in the afternoon, so I can forgive him."

Henrie asked him if he was serious, and he only had to show her his cell phone to prove to her that they'd slept nearly twenty hours straight after going to bed last night at around eight-thirty. No wonder she felt so good. A great night's sleep like she'd had would do that for a person.

Trevor started to strip down, and when he was naked, he joined her anyway in the tub, sitting behind her in the large area and helping her wash up her arms. She knew on some level there was more to tell her, but like he seemed to be doing, she didn't want to rush it.

"You remember me telling you about the kid? Her name was Debra when we first encountered her, but her real name was Lavender." She said that she remembered them telling her that she was in prison. "Not really a prison but a place that made it so that she would never escape, nor would anyone be around to talk to her. She was killed this afternoon, just after one o'clock." She turned and looked at him.

"I wouldn't imagine that it was just her being killed that had him calling you. Something else happened." He nodded and poured shampoo into his hand, and washed her hair. "Tell me, please. If not, I'm going to think of all kinds of things that might have happened with her dying. Did she kill anyone?"

"Yes, her guard." Reaching for the plastic cup that she'd been using on her hair, he rinsed it out of all the shampoo. "They would drop things into her cell from an opening in the top of the cell. It wasn't a large hole, and it was a good twenty feet from the floor, too. Her food was given to her by a slot that was only big enough to slide the tray into the side of her prison, and that was all. When the man who was working the shift dropped her down some extra blankets that she asked for, she had somehow made her way up to the hold and grabbed him. There wasn't any way for her to get out of the cell, but she pulled him in over and over until he was decapitated and died." She sat up again and looked at Trevor, asking him to finish the story. "One of the other guards saw what was happening but was too late to get help to the other man. What he did do was drag the body out of the opening and fire down into the opening until he could see that she was dead."

"Was she?" Trevor told her that they wouldn't open the cell for a week, watching her every move to make sure that she wasn't faking her death. "If not, then they'd go in, retrieve her body, and bury her on the land that surrounds the facility."

"She had no family, I take it." Trevor told her that any family that she'd had was dead as far as she was concerned, and if there was family, they'd never know what happened to her anyway. That's the reason for the cell that she was in. "It's kind of frightening. Don't you think that they have those cells for a reason? I mean, how many are out there, and are there a lot of them all over the United States?"

"I don't know, and yes, they're all over the country. Just for people like her, who seem to have no conscious for what they do or how they do it." She shivered and asked him if it would ever come back on them that they had a part in her being locked up. "No. The only reason that Maverick knows is because he was watching the area. While he didn't see it, he knew who to call to find out what happened. There will be nothing saying that she died now how she was killed. No obit in the paper. The place where she'll be buried will not have a marker nor a headstone to mark who had passed and how. She didn't exist so far as anyone is concerned."

No more was said about Lavender or whatever her name was. They soaked in the tub for a while until the water got too cold. After getting out of the bath, they dressed and decided to get some dinner and find them each a car. She thought that it was the perfect way to spend black Friday with all the stores going crazy. Then, it occurred to her that it was almost Christmas, and she didn't know if they had a single ornament between them. She didn't even know if they celebrated Christmas or did they go all out. So many things that she didn't know about her new family that would make or break the holidays.

Glad that they talked on the way to Columbus. The weather had turned to a warm forty degrees, making the roads slushy and dangerous. But most of the highways were cleared off and it was easy going for the two of them. As soon as they were off the highway and into Columbus, the roads were perfectly clear there as well.

"This year, my brother is going to host Christmas. Clay and Lizzy were living in the family home and wanted to be the first to have all of them over. Jenson and Jade would be late in coming as they had political things that needed them to be present, and then they were going to DC to have dinner with the president." She'd not realized that they knew the man, and it turned out that Jade was the godmother to the president's oldest child at ten years old.

While in town, the two of them picked up some decorations to do the house in as well as a large tree that would be in their living room. She was able to get everything delivered to their home by calling in a couple of her own favors and one of the drivers that worked for Banister and Banister — B&B would pick them up on his way back to the offices and have them delivered. It was the most fun she'd had shopping, knowing that she'd not have to carry things to the car and then drive home with an overstuffed vehicle.

Not only did they get a great many ornaments for the tree but the two of them picked up some gifts for the family as well. When it was getting dark out, they decided to stay in town to do some more shopping in the morning. B&B was closed the weekend and wouldn't open again until Tuesday of next week. Then, after Christmas, it would be closed from two days before the holiday until the Monday after the New Year's. Christmas bonuses would have been shipped out the week before Thanksgiving, giving them enough time to make arrangements for their own holiday shopping.

They had to call some of the family to ask for things that the children had wanted. Like most people that had a new family they were going all out. The twins were the only ones that they'd been given a list with, and it was only gift cards to places that sold books and other items that babies would like things from. Still, they purchased them both a gift and were glad that they'd been told that they don't dress alike but similar.

She'd never had this much fun buying gifts for people. Her grandparents, of course, but there hadn't been anyone else in her life that she wanted to go all out for. For their drivers, they gave them bonuses and time off with pay for the holidays. However, this was something new to her, and she thought that when the kids came around, they'd be shopping from the day after Christmas until the next holiday. Being with her family this season was going to be epic. And she couldn't wait to enjoy her familie's and have so much fun. Yes, she thought, the holidays were going to be so much more fun.

~*~

Trevor was about as excited as he'd ever been. They'd been out and about all day and now they were having a nice dinner in one of the most posh restaurants in the city. Having a steak and all the trimmings, he was happy that Henrie had decided that she wanted seafood and had gotten a lobster tail with warm butter, too. They could barely eat. They were touching each other above and below the table. They'd even had a delicious wine to go with their meals.

"I heard from the drivers. Your brother showed up and let them in the house just fine, and they've made sure that everything is locked up so that no one gets in. Also, he checked on my grandparents while there, and he said that they were doing just fine, having a good time." Trevor asked her if they were aware of what was going on with the delivery. "I don't think so. He said they thought it was just furniture that was being delivered and told them not to scrape the floors. This is the most fun I've had in ages."

"Me too. I mean, not just buying things, I've never done that before, but just the sneaking around that we've been able to do." Their salads were brought to them, and they ate them while going over the gifts they'd already been able to take care of. "I'm glad you thought of that cruise for my parents. I think they'll love it."

"They deserve it. I know that they've had one a few years ago and I know that your mom has been hinting around to your father about going." Trevor told her that his dad wasn't one to take hints all that well. "That's what your mom said. She said that what she'd do normally was to go ahead and book things for them and then later, closer to whatever they were going to do was to tell him then. Then he'd act like it was all his idea."

"Your dad is brilliant but befuddled most of the time. I think that it has something to do with keeping up with all of you boys." Trevor told her that he was sure that was it. "I've never seen a man that loves his wife as much as he does. Other than us. But he almost worships her. It's kind of nice, I think."

"My parents have always been in love, I think. Dad would buy Mom flowers because it was the twelfth of the month. Or take her out to a movie because he wanted her to see something that he knew she'd like. It didn't matter if it wasn't something that he'd enjoy, he told me once. It was because he knew that she would." She asked him about flowers. "Mom was never one to enjoy cut flowers. When they died, she was heartbroken, and it bothered him. So, each year, around the first part of spring, he would buy her a living bloom. Not necessarily roses, though she does love them, but he would buy her something that she could plant and watch it grow. He'd tell her his love for her. He's very romantic. Forgetful at times, but he is the one that taught us how to treat a woman that you love."

"I'll have to thank him later. I love you." He told Henrie that he loved her as well. "I never in my wildest dreams thought that I'd ever find love. Not like this, anyway. I always thought that I might settle for someone later when I was too old to change my ways and just live with him because I didn't have time to mess with someone new in my life. But that's not true of you. I find that I want to spend time with you. And if we live to be a hundred years old, it's doubtful to me that we'd ever get bored with each other." Trevor said that she was a romantic, too. "Because of you."

They were finished with dinner at around seven. Since it was too cold to do much in the way of walking around, the two of them headed back to their hotel. He'd never been so glad for a limo to pick them up as he was that night.

The weather had turned nasty again and neither of them was looking forward to driving home tomorrow. The cars that they had picked out were four-wheel drive but it still made Henrie nervous driving. He promised her that they were in no hurry and that if she had to stop for any reason, even just to relax a bit, he would as well since they had nothing but time on their hands.

There had been a horrific accident on the road when they were just outside of Zanesville. It took them longer than he thought to get around it and by the time they were home, they were both exhausted. He knew that it was because of the harrowing experience of driving in the snow, but he also knew that it had stressed Henrie out more because of the wreck. He was never so happy to see their driveway as they pulled up in front of the house. Getting inside, he was glad for the furnace and the warm living room. Sitting down on the couch, he nearly swallowed his tongue when Henrie sat on his lap facing him.

Pulling off her jeans, he watched her as they were dropped on the floor. It was then that he noticed that she wasn't wearing any panties. Nor he'd noticed all night was she wearing a bra. Every part of him seemed to wake up and was ready for anything that she wanted.

"You could kill a man doing this to him when he's stressed out." She moved to sit on the couch next to him after taking off her blouse. Then he knelt down on the floor in front of her. Putting her legs on either side of his body, he pulled her to the end of the couch and leaned down to her wet, warm entrance. "Come for me, Henrie. Come for me so that I can taste all that you are."

Licking her from gate to clit, he slid his tongue deep inside of her. He was rewarded with a flood of cream so thick and wonderfully flavorful that he couldn't stop taking as much as he possibly could from her. Her moans were enough to make him come on his own, but he wanted her pleasure before he had his own.

Trevor had no idea how long he had eaten her — it felt not nearly long enough, but when she jerked his head up from her by grabbing his hair, he could see the lust on her face. There was love, too. Shining as brightly from her eyes as he hoped his did to her.

"Take me, Trevor. Fill me before I come again." He sat up from her, pulling her off the couch and onto his cock. She screamed, falling backward onto the couch as she continued to scream over and over in her release. "Come with me, please? I need you to come with me and give me a climax that takes me away."

Rolling to the floor, he took her. It had been his idea to make love to her gently, but she wasn't having it. Nor was he. Fucking her hard, no other word for it, he slammed in and out of her even as she came again and again.

When his own climax took him, starting at his cock and spreading all over his body hard and fast, he knew that this woman was going to kill him with sex. Trevor felt his eyes roll to the back of his head and dizziness roll over him. His body stiffened, the pounding of his heart so violent that he was sure that it was going to come from his chest. As his body was reaching the pinnacle, he came again. Hurting this time, he cried out. When he was finally spent, more than he'd ever been in his life, he fell atop of Henrie and lay there.

"You're too heavy." Henrie giggled then. "Please, Trevor, you need to roll over before you murder me. I can feel your cock still moving, and it's making me have these little heart-palpating kinds of climaxes."

He rolled them both over with the last of his strength. When she giggled again, he opened one eye. That's all he could muster right now, and he glared as best he could at her. Not that it mattered. She had closed her eyes and looked to be sound asleep. Adjusting her around so that they were both comfortable, he closed his eyes as well and let sleep and the long day take him under.

He had no idea what time it was when Henrie shook him awake. Pulling on his jeans, not bothering with zipping them up, they made their way to their bedroom. Tomorrow, their hot tub was coming, and he couldn't wait. Getting the kinks out of his body from having sex a great deal more than he'd ever had, Trevor knew that if he got any more relaxed than he was right now, he'd be dead. There was no doubt in his mind that sex was the best relaxant that he'd ever experienced.

The bed was nice and cool. He had no idea why, but he enjoyed getting into a cool or cold bed year-round. There was an electric blanket on it but he never used his. Snuggling up to Henrie when she was warm would cause her to squeal and smack him, but he didn't care. He held her to him until he was warm, too.

The next morning, he got up before Henrie.

He was going to allow her to sleep as long as she wanted as he took a shower and got ready for the day. There were boxes of items that had been delivered, and he wanted to get a start on them right away. The tree could wait until Henrie got up as he wanted to make sure that they both decorated their tree this first year. It made him wonder if, by this time next year, they'd have a child and smiled. Children. He wanted as many as Henrie wanted.

By the time she'd come to join him in the dining room—where he was putting things that needed to be wrapped, he'd been able to unearth the wrapping paper that they'd gotten, as well as tape and scissors. As soon as she said the word, they'd be ready.

"You didn't put the tree up?" Trevor explained to her his reason for not tackling the big job. "That's so sweet of you. I love it. We'll have our first of many Christmases this year, and I can't wait."

The two of them spent nearly three hours on just putting the tree together and into the corner where they wanted it shown off in. He knew that they'd bought a tall tree, but he'd not counted on it taking forever to put together. Getting out the few ornaments that they'd gotten, it was looking more and more festive as they hung them on the branches.

Henrie was making a list of things that they needed, too. There were plenty of lights to cover the tree, but they'd forgotten to get the little hangers for ornaments. They also needed an extension cord to plug in the train set that was going to be surrounding the tree when it was finished.

They also decided that they wanted a big wreath for the front door as well as a smaller tree for their dining room. Neither of them thought that it would get used overly much but they wanted the house to be festive as they could make it. Also, the kitchen. She wanted to decorate it as well since they took most of their meals in there.

By the time they were finished up, the hot tub had arrived. Putting it off from their bedroom seemed to be the smartest thing to do, and it would keep others from getting into it if they were gone. He'd never seen it himself, but he'd heard of people using their neighbor's pool and hot tub while they were out of town and trashing things up. While he didn't think that would happen with them, he was taking no chances.

After having a light lunch and then a big supper, both of them were ready to go back to bed. However they did have to get some of the presents wrapped up so that no one would see them if they just happened by. Trevor thought that the excitement of being able to surprise his family this year was the most fun.

Years before, he would just get his brothers whatever they told him they wanted. No more. He'd had the most fun picking out Jenson's gift. They'd found a gavel and had his name put on it. It didn't seem like much, but he knew that Jenson would get a kick out of it. And for Clay, they'd gotten him a miniature Land Rover because of all the work he'd been doing since taking over NASA. Things like that for each of them that while not costly, they were meaningful.

That night, they were able to get into the hot tub and relax. He thought for sure that Henrie was going to have to use a scoop to get him out of it. His body was nothing but limp muscles by the time they were ready for bed. He was nearly asleep, standing up when he was in the bedroom and into the bed.

Chapter 8

In a short twelve years since he and Henrie had been married, so many things had changed. Holding his daughter in his arms after feeding her the bottle, he marveled at the fact that he was a father again. He and Henrie had four boys and this little girl. Lisa Marie Strong was going to be spoiled rotten if the way her brothers were falling all over themselves in caring for her.

Jenson was due home tonight with Jade and their brood. Jade had been nearly eight months pregnant when he decided to run for the presidency. When he'd come into a close second to winning, it made him work all the harder to win the seat the following years. Not only did Jenson win by a landslide, his second term was no different.

His brother had had the highest popularity vote of any president before him, including Brock Wisecarver, their former president and great friend of the family. Jade had had the first child born in the White House in decades, and the little man had grown up telling people that he was going to be president someday, too. Trevor believed him.

The party they were having for his parents had been planned for months, and the send-off on a cruise was going to be so good for them. At last count they had nearly twenty grandchildren with more on the way. Mom and Dad hated to leave when they had so much fun with them that they wouldn't take a break unless they were out of town. His parents were so loving that he was sure that the kids would rather be with them than their own parents.

Lizzy had given birth to two sets of twins, all boys. She was going to be hard to get away from their little Lisa when she was away. Clay and her loved their boys very much, but they had so wanted a girl this time around. He'd bet anything that they'd have more children, at least until they decided that boys were all they'd get.

Clay still worked for NASA. He'd made so many changes to the program that he'd been voted best boss by his team four years in a row. People were clamoring to get into his department and even kids that he'd been around in their town were saying that they were going to work for Clay. There were women working for the firm now and hadn't been before. It was quite a feather in his hat too for women voters for Jenson as well that his little brother was so good at hiring anyone that qualified rather than just making it an *all-boys* club like it had been before.

It amazed him that Barkley and Carrie had gone on to have several children. Their oldest two, identical twin girls had been adopted by them about fifteen years ago. They'd grown up about as secure and healthy as any children had been when he considered how they'd started out in life.

Sunny and Bethany, at only a few months old had been abused by their grandparents in the most unusual way. It turned out that Michael Cartwright had been their father too, having an affair with Mick's wife. It was a sorted tale and one that no one talked about anymore. Sunny was doing well in her academics and Bethany wanted to be a child psychologist.

Carrie, Barkley's wife was the sister to the children's mother. She nor the other family had had anything to do with their sister Matty for a long time. It was horrible the way that Matty treated them all. And now she was dead along with her mother-in-law.

Barton's family didn't grow like the others.

After having their one and only child, they devoted all their time to helping families get on the right track with children with special needs. Not just children with needs as in being handicapped, but children that were brilliant beyond anything that people had seen and helping them adjust like their own son had done. Sherm was brilliant, beyond any scope that anyone had ever seen yet he was bullied at schools where he was a teenager and all the kids in his classes in college were older and meaner. It had worked out well for all of them and the best part was, Sherm had gone on to helping others too. He'd become a doctor at a very young age and the entire family was very proud of him. Their little girl, Hanna, worshipped her brother and hung out with him wherever he was. It was a great family dynamic.

Barton worked with children as well. Getting over phobias like Sherm had had when he'd been younger. He still feared water, a large expanse of it, and sometimes had to work through his fear when playing in the pool, thanks mainly to do with Lorie, Toria's sister, being the bitch that she'd been.

Then there was Lavender. Lavender had been staying with Jenson and his wife for a few days when it was found out that her guardian, ninety-year-old LeAnn, had passed away. They took her in to make sure that she was given a good home but she'd turned out to be a murderer and a sadist. It made him shiver every time he thought about her and her methods of killing people.

Maverick was the happiest he thought of all his brothers. He had a wonderful wife in Gracie and they also had the most children. It was funny that his older brother had had the set of twins that were a girl and a boy. He wondered too if there was ever a child in the little town that went to bed hungry with the two of them looking after them.

They ran soup kitchens right out of their home. Would supply money for college aged kids that were struggling with both working and trying to study. They would do this under the cover of just helping out when in fact it saved a great many family and children from having to drop out of college in order to pay for things such as books or just meeting the electric bill payment before having their power turned off. He loved all his brothers but he was especially close to Maverick and his wife Gracie. They were so modest that it made him love them even more.

He and Henrie had a good life as well.

They were living in their home with all their kids surrounding them. From their first Christmas it had been trying to outdo the one before. Not with gifts, no, the family got enough gifts from them but with décor. Their house was the one to go and see at all holidays but they specially loved Christmas. Even Halloween was a big to do and people from miles away would come by and see what they had put up every year.

"Dad?" He turned to look at his son, asking him if everything was all right. "Yeah, sure. I have a problem at school. Well, it's not my problem but one of the guys I have in my class. I think that he's living alone in his apartment."

"What makes you think that?" He told him some of the things that he'd been asking him about. "Just because he didn't know how to use a washer doesn't make him alone in the world. You know how because your mother and I wanted to make sure you could care for yourself if you were every left alone."

"Yeah, but you never leave any of us alone." He asked if he could hold his sister. After setting him up with her, he didn't move far away just in case he got tried of her. Not that he could see that happening but he didn't want to take any chances.

"Lisa is beautiful, don't you think, Dad?"

"I do. Now, tell me what you're thinking about your friend." He asked him not to get mad at him. "Never. You've been helping him out, I understand that but what is it that you think I'm going to be mad at you about?"

"I've been giving him my lunch. You have that thing set up at school so that I can buy my lunch when I want to so I've been using that. The teachers won't let him set up the account on account of him being so far behind in his payments from last year. Now his little sister is going to school, which I didn't know until yesterday and they neither one can eat there. I wonder if he's got anything at home to feed them." Trevor asked his son if he knew that he was alone or was he guessing. "I know it. A week ago I walked home so that I could go by his house. When I got there, there wasn't any cars in the driveway nor was anyone mowing their lawn. It's really big now, the grass I mean."

"All good observations and no, I'm not mad at you for making it so that your friend can eat. I bet he also saves some of his food you give him to take to his sister." His son nodded. "All right, what is it that you want to do? I know you don't want to embarrass them so you tell me what you've worked out in getting you some answers."

"He's afraid that someone is going to catch him and separate his sister from him. He said that she was all he had." He asked him how long did he think this was going on. "Weeks and weeks. I should have told you sooner but he asked me not to. And he's my friend and I didn't want to tattle on him. But…well Dad, he's really sick. So is his little sister but not as bad as he is. All he does is cough and cough until the teacher sends him to the office. I don't think she likes him all that much because sometimes he'd dirty and other times he's sleeping. He told me that he stays awake at night trying to do his homework by candle. Their power got turned off a while ago and now he's afeared that the water will be turned off and they won't have anything to wash up with. That might have already happened. He's been coming to school with dirty clothes again."

"Put your sister in bed there and we'll go over there. You can tell him that you were extra worried for them and I'll take it from there. And I'm also going to have your grandda go over there to the school and find out why no one reported him for having no food at lunchtime. We set up a fund there that he and his sister can use anytime they need it. It's not right that they aren't getting the food they need." He asked him again if he was mad. "Never, I told you this. I'm very proud of you for thinking of him and making sure that he had something to eat. Very proud."

After telling Henrie where they were going, she handed him some cash that she'd gotten from the bank to take to the school and made sure that there was enough to pay up their fines and a lunch ticket. She was spitting mad but she also told him how proud she was of him. He loved his wife so much, in that moment.

It didn't take them long to get to the house. And just as his son had said, the grass was overgrown and there was a notice for it to be taken care of by the police. The health department had left a note too saying that anyone living in the house was to vacate as there was no power and they had to get out. As soon as he knocked on the door, the little boy opened it and the look of complete fear on his face startled him enough that he pulled him out of the house and told the two boys to wait until he came out with the little girl. He walked into seeing the little girl being tied to a chair and it looked like they were going to beat her.

Kathi S. Barton

"Who the hell are you?" He told them and why he was there. "So what? Where is that idiot boy of ours? He's supposed to keep up the house and just look at this mess he left. And the power is off. Should have gotten him a job to pay it off instead of talking to people that don't got any never mind to be talking to."

Trevor wasn't sure what the man meant but he untied the little girl and sent her out. But not before having to knock the woman out for trying to get at her. He leaned down to the girl while she was sobbing and told her to tell the boys to go to his house with her and have Henrie call the police. She ran out of the house so quickly he hoped that she'd stop long enough to gather up the other two.

He was smiling at that thought when he faced the parents. "Where have you been for the last several weeks?" They told him that they'd been in Vegas having some fun and he didn't have it right, they said, they'd been there for four months. "You left two small children alone and without food in the house, not to mention power in their home for four months? What the hell is wrong with you?"

When his cell phone rang he knew that it was Jenson. Having found out so quickly what he was doing more than likely had to do more with his wife than him hearing about it on the news. As soon as the front door burst open, he took the call from the president of the US, his big brother.

"Henrie called me." That was enough for him to laugh. "Laugh it up little brother but don't be surprised if you've adopted two more children by the end of the day."

"Gladly." He told him that he figured he'd say that. "I hope that whomever is coming into the house now is someone you sent?"

"It's the calvary."

Sure enough it was who he said. Not only were there FBI agents in the room with him but the welfare department, the police — it seemed like all of them as well as the secret Service men that would go with any of the family when they were out and about. There were more of them than he'd seen in one place in some time. Glad they were on his side, Trevor let them handle the couple while he made his way home to see to the kids. He shouldn't have worried.

Not only were they in clean clothing but had had a bath, washed their hair and were eating a sandwich at the counter in the kitchen. Kissing Henrie, his most wonderful partner and wife, he asked the kids what they wanted for supper. There was no doubt in his mind that not only would they be watching over the kids from now on, but they'd also have two more Strongs in the family too. His life couldn't have been better than it was right now. And he'd not change a single thing about it.

Before You Go...

HELP AN AUTHOR

write a review

THANK YOU!

Share your voice and help guide other readers to these wonderful books. Even if it's only a line or two, your reviews help readers discover the author's books so they can continue creating stories that you'll love. Log in to your favorite retailer and leave a review. Thank you.

AWARD WINNING, BESTSELLING AUTHOR

Kathi Barton, a winner of the Pinnacle Book Achievement Award and a best-selling author on Amazon and All Romance books, lives in Nashport, Ohio, with her husband, Paul. When not creating new worlds and romance, Kathi and her husband enjoy camping and going to auctions. She can also be seen at county fairs with her husband, an artist and potter.

Her muse, a cross between Jimmy Stewart and Hugh Jackman, brings her stories to life for her readers in a way that has them coming back time and again for more. Her favorite genre is paranormal romance, with a great deal of spice. You can visit Kathi online and drop her an email if you'd like. She loves hearing from her fans. aaronskiss@gmail.com.

Follow Kathi on her blog: http://kathisbartonauthor.blogspot.com/

www.ingramcontent.com/pod-product-compliance
Lightning Source LLC
Chambersburg PA
CBHW031958170626
46807CB00006B/2548